Metaphorosis

July 2020

Beautifully made speculative fiction

Also from Metaphorosis

Verdage

Reading 5X5 x2: Duets
Score – an SFF symphony
Reading 5X5: Readers' Edition
Reading 5X5: Writers' Edition

Metaphorosis Magazine

Metaphorosis: Best of 20xx
Metaphorosis 20xx: The Complete Stories
annual issues, from 2016

Monthly issues

Plant Based Press

Best Vegan Science Fiction & Fantasy
annual issues, from 2016

from B. Morris Allen:
Susurrus
Allenthology: Volume I
Tocsin: and other stories
Start with Stones: collected stories
Metaphorosis: a collection of stories

Metaphorosis

July 2020

edited by
B. Morris Allen

ISSN: 2573-136X (online)
ISBN: 978-1-64076-173-5 (e-book)
ISBN: 978-1-64076-174-2 (paperback)

Metaphorosis
a magazine of speculative fiction
from
Metaphorosis Publishing

Neskowin

July 2020

The Friendly Ghost

Ashley R. Carlson

A Year Before

Conversations with you were never dull (it was one of the main reasons I wanted to marry you), but that night things had taken a random turn from flirty innuendos and our cat's sudden-onset sneezing attacks to more macabre fare.

You'd just told me about a dangerous incident that happened on the work site, and that if things had been left running a *little* while longer, you could've lost a limb or worse from exploding shrapnel.

I'm probably not gonna make it past sixty, you texted, before insisting that 'when' you died before I did, I had to remain in lifelong mourning and embrace celibacy wholeheartedly. I told you that was ridiculous—on numerous counts—because our parents were older than that already, spry in that middle-class, Boomer way that propelled them haughtily on through retirement, golfing and brunching and perpetually driving five miles under the speed limit wherever they went.

Well if I die first, I'm going to haunt you, I joked. The text exchange was one of thousands we'd shared during our year-long marriage and two years of dating before that. They were a godsend to me, those (usually) cheerful blue bubbles coming in spurts (interspersed with the occasional NSFW Snapchat pic), to offer a comforting, digital tether for the two weeks of every month when work took you out of state.

Don't even say that.

It could happen, Dan! Don't live in denial! And I'm nice, because I want you to get remarried and everything.

It better not, and I wouldn't. But fine, I guess you can haunt me. Just promise you'll be a friendly ghost.

What, exactly, is a 'friendly' ghost? I munched on a Milano cookie as I typed, pausing my reality show on the flat-screen —a show you unwaveringly refused to watch because of the cast members' 'arguments about a chihuahua named Lucy Lucy Apple Juice' that comprised most of the season's overarching plotline. I had this sudden craving to know what sort of ghost you'd deem 'tolerable,' and added another message to our text stream —the ghost emoji, draped in white with its tongue stuck out, arms raised in mid-scare. *Boo! I see you. Do you see me?* it implied, a lighthearted caricature of the real thing for kids and still-honeymoon-phasing couples to send one another on Halloween.

One who helps the person they haunt.

What, like in the movie Ghost, *with Patrick Swayze? For justice and all that?* I texted, digging in the bag for another Milano and coming up empty with a disgruntled sigh; reality shows always made me ravenous. They were a modern-day, gluttonous feast of drama and intrigue, except that the fighters in the arena had been replaced by diamond-draped, viper-tongued housewives.

No, not like that, you replied. I could almost hear you utter it aloud, the threat of sorrow deepening the tenor of your voice, one normally so animated with jest. The topic had edged into depressing territory, especially when we were a thousand miles apart.

Then what? I typed, still acutely curious of your definition, for this was a page as-yet-unturned in the book that was your thoughts and feelings. *What kind of ghost would you like me to be?*

Maybe you'd been called away from your phone to tend to an issue on the construction site, or a manager had come into the office and scowled to find the team's star supervisor engrossed in his phone at the start of another nightshift—but you didn't respond for a while, and by then I'd finished my show, tucked the cat in, and lay curled under the covers of the king-size bed we shared only part time.

I promise, baby, I texted to conclude the discussion, for I knew you well, and while you were the epitome of showy masculine verve—you lived to lift weights at the gym, used gag-inducing "bro"-ish terms too often for me to count, and could grill up a perfectly smoked brisket in your sleep—you were the more sensitive of the two of us; your center was ooey-gooey, and I had to be careful not to jostle your insides while you were away. *I'd be a friendly ghost*, I asserted via text, and that was it, followed by a quick *goodnight, I love you so much!!!!* with lots of exclamation points because you liked them. Tomorrow we'd resume our conversation on those benign issues between newly married couples—paycheck amounts and which bills were coming up next, small health concerns centered around bowel regularity that kept us laughing and did much to close the gap of physical space between us in one perfectly timed poop emoji.

I'm happy to say that all these months later, I've kept my promise.

A Week After

It's my funeral today, but goddamn if it doesn't look like yours.

It's awful to see you like this—eyes as bruised underneath as over-ripe plums, thick dark hair gelled to one side by the budget-salon stylist you visited this morning at the request of your mother (and I'm thankful she insisted, because you haven't washed it yourself in nearly a week). I've only ever seen you looking this haggard once before, following our first and only separation eight months into the relationship, when I still wasn't sure we were right for each other. I'd showed up right after a long, expletive-and-tear-filled post-breakup phone call, because I missed you and it stung to hear you so distraught. As I walked up that narrow sidewalk to find you in the suffocating heat of midsummer twilight, the way your wilted stance against the doorway made me ache was evidence enough that regardless of our differences, I was deeply in love and never wanted to let you go again.

This hurts too—worse, because back then I'd chosen to separate from you, something I could (and swiftly did) remedy. These circumstances are unequivocally more permanent.

Your eulogy is nice, if a little short, and you don't cry. You haven't much, and it's concerning, but not because I'm worried you don't care. There's a place inside that I think you've gone to, burrowed deep, deep down to hide, even deeper than that time I ended it and you said on the phone you hadn't been able to sleep or eat properly in weeks, and didn't really see the point in changing that. You need someone to coax you from that insidious, inviting darkness before it seeps in and poisons you to the bone—and I'm not going anywhere until I lead you out.

I promised.

Two Weeks After

I'm still learning the rules of being a ghost.

You shiver if I touch you, but that's about it. You only seem to hear me at night while you're sleeping, and every time I've whispered "I love you" and "I'm going to help you through this," you've just moaned or whimpered, as if the mere lilt of my voice is a minor but still very present kind of torture.

I wander the house once you're asleep —wary of the glowing doorway that appears in the corner of every room I enter, softly lit along the edges of the closed door and inviting me to approach, but never demanding it.

I visit with the cat instead, who can definitely still see me based on the way his protuberant eyes follow me in the dark, wary and appraising, as if he's forgotten I was his beloved caretaker mere weeks ago. Maybe I look different; maybe my ghostly form has retained the gruesome injuries sustained during my death, and they frighten him. For all I know, an array of lacerations still spider-webs across my forehead, a bit of exposed gristle hanging where the truck burst through the driver's side to split the lower part of my face in half. There's no reflection in the mirror to confirm this, but when I run my fingertip across my chin, its journey is reassuringly smooth.

I don't need sleep or sustenance, but I'm able to perch on furniture well enough, and can even turn the TV on if I slam my hand against the remote enough times. It took me more than an hour to get the damn thing to work playing the latest episode of my favorite show—you haven't dismantled the DVR preferences yet, though when I was alive you bemoaned the fact that our limited recording space was always full of bullshit squabbles in fancy restaurants and phony attempts at finding the 'one'. These shows give me comfort in the silent hours of the night when you finally find rest—what I hope to be *true* rest, not the hours spent catatonic in bed until your mom or mine shows up and forces you to eat some of their homemade empanadas and pozole, before busying themselves with gathering up the growing, untouched pile of dirty laundry strewn about the house and momentarily freezing when they find a pair of my socks or underwear in the fray, before hurriedly tossing them in the washer with the rest.

It's not long before the cat joins me on the couch for our nightly viewings, moving between you in the bedroom and me on the sofa to purr and knead the thick, wooly blanket we used to nestle under for *Game of Thrones* marathons—a child in the midst of two parents separated by far more than divorce.

One Month After

You are acting strange.

I notice it first when you call your boss and quit out of the blue, even though they've been exceptionally understanding about it all, offering three months' worth of paid leave following the funeral.

It's when you try to give the cat to your parents that I realize my nightly stream of encouragements beside you in bed haven't ameliorated your grief in the least.

"I don't want him anymore," you slur on the phone, a full tumbler of whiskey in hand. You've been drinking all day, unaware of my reprimands to at least *eat* something between aggressively thrown-back shots of liquor. "He was hers. I don't fucking *want* him! I HATE THIS FUCKING CAT AND I DON'T WANT TO CLEAN UP HIS SHIT ANYMORE!" you bellow into the receiver.

That's a complete lie—I know it, you know it, for god's sakes, the cat knows it. He's scowling at you right now, having just left you another smelly gift in his litterbox.

Whatever your mom says on the other end sets you off. You shout again and throw the phone at the wall hard enough to shatter the screen, before storming into the hallway toward the medicine cabinet.

"What are you doing?" I cry as I follow you, watching as you rummage through the bottles of ibuprofen and Midol and Sudafed with trembling fingers.

You pivot and stride through me to return to the kitchen. Reach for a glass from the cabinet and fill it with water from the sink.

"What the fuck are you *doing*?!" I repeat as you fumble with the childproof lid on the bottle. "Hey! Stop it right now! *Stop!*"

I slam into you and it's like fighting against wind, like passing my hands through a cloud of smoke for all the difference it makes. You've got a palmful of round orange pills now, at least three dozen, and you're bringing them to your lips with a hand that's suddenly steadier than I've seen in weeks. I scream so loud and shrilly that it frightens the cat and he's off like a shot under the couch, but you're undeterred, they're in your mouth now, you're about to chase them down with water—

"DANIEL HERNANDEZ, YOU STOP IT *RIGHT FUCKING NOW!*"

My shriek shatters a nearby trio of glass bottles full of seashells we gathered on a Puerto Rican trip to celebrate our first wedding anniversary, splinters of blue-green glass and shells exploding across the kitchen table in all directions.

It also breaks the glass in your hand.

You stand there, stunned, bare feet strewn with fragmented glass, bottom lip split and bleeding from an errant slice. You bend over the sink and spit the pills out, a hunk of saliva-slicked half-white, half-orange rounds, and back away to survey the mess.

Your brown eyes are wary, wide.

You say my name—*mouth* it, soundlessly. Like a prayer.

You finally start to cry, torso-shattering sobs that bring you to the kitchen floor. I bend to take you in my arms, forgetting for a moment you can't feel a thing.

Eleven Months After

You've just returned to your new apartment from the gym, sipping on a protein shake. You've been lifting at this new gym a lot recently, and it shows in the supple sinews of your back and arms, the renewed vibrancy of your light brown skin.

It's all new, as if scouring me from your surroundings will also scour me from your memories: apartment, city, job, furniture, clothes. You sold the house, donated our stuff to charity, got a new position in another state—but you kept the cat. I encouraged each step, talking to you day and night about why you should stay alive, how much more there was for you to do. A fresh start was what you needed and what you got, but all that newness didn't mean I was ready to leave. You were still alone (the cat didn't count), and I'd decided that in order to *really* make it better—to live up to my promise—you deserved a full life with someone new.

I was concerned about a forced disconnection before my goal was achieved; perhaps I was bound to the *house* and not you, and when you drove off I'd have to say goodbye for good and finally go through the doorway I'd staunchly been avoiding for nearly a year.

On the day you packed your few remaining belongings and set off with the cat for the big city and the new job, I waited in front of the house, watching until your car's red brake lights were only an echo, a smeared corona when I shut my eyes; a ghost of what had once been concrete, been *there*. I paced the driveway, ignoring that damned glowing doorway ever-present in the corner of my vision.

"I'm not ready yet! *He's* not ready yet! Fuck off!" I finally hollered at the door, and it shrank and shrank, to the size of a doggie door and then a mousehole and then a pinprick, until it winked out completely for the first time since the car crash.

I paced that driveway in your absence, searching my memory for how I'd gotten from that fluorescent-bathed hospital room to the funeral and back to the house, but I truly couldn't recall.

It wasn't too long before I *did* end up where you and the cat were, suddenly going all misty like vapor passing between someone's lips on a cold night, only to come together again in your new apartment just in time to see you shuffling inside with the cat carrier and a suitcase.

"So I do haunt *you*, then," I said, thoroughly relieved. I still had a lot left to do.

A Year and Nine Months After

You're checking yourself out in the bathroom mirror, and I laugh.

"I *told* you you'd start losing your hair one day," I say as you gather a bit of gel in your palm and attempt to wrestle your brown strands into a coif that somewhat hides the thinning at your temples and crown. You've got a date tonight, the first since I died, and I'm not trying to be a brat, but she looks a bit... *basic*. That's my jealousy talking, I know—I was the one who prompted you about this online dating stuff anyway, murmuring in your ear night after night to make sure you heard me. But then you went and matched with some Basic Blonde who looks nothing like me and wore a goddamn bathing suit in every single one of her pictures (if you can call a strip of fabric up your ass-crack a suit), so your selection has me questioning whether this was all a huge mistake.

While you're gone I putter around the apartment, tidying up in ways I know from experience you won't notice. I'm watching the latest housewife mayhem when you start to unlock the front door, and I manage to turn the TV off just in time to see you tripping over the apartment's threshold with the Basic Blonde in tow.

"Christ, you're drunk," I mutter as you fumble for the light switch and quickly give up on finding it. "Better not have driven home—" I stop myself there; you've done a few questionable things since my death, but committing the very same act my killer did isn't one of them.

Without preamble, BB yanks you toward your bedroom. You leave the room's door open—no one lives here but you and the cat, right?—so I'm forced to listen to what happens next, glancing every so often at the ethereal doorway to my right with a sneer (it reappeared a few weeks back, just as incandescent and pleasant-looking as ever).

"This isn't *exactly* what I meant when I said you should start dating again," I chide, watching the cat vacillate between licking his butt and peering sympathetically in my direction.

When it's over, the blonde has the audacity to think it's time to talk. I waltz into the bedroom and lean against the wall—this is too rich a conversation to miss.

"So," she begins, spread-eagled on the mattress beside you. She's pretty (if generic) in person, and this irritates me to an unexpected degree. I snarl in her direction, and the drapes nearby ripple. "Am I the first?"

"What?" you say, breathless, but already sobering up, by the sound of it.

"Am I the first since...you know."

"Oh, Jesus Christ," I snort, crossing my arms like I'm hugging myself, but it's really because I'm filling up with rage—a rage I've never felt before, a *poltergeist* level of rage. "You *told* her? This chick? Really?"

You squint in disbelief. It must be the alcohol that's loosened your tongue, because you actually respond to her moronic inquiry. "Y-yeah. You are."

"Nice." She says it as if she's won a prize, and I mean yes, you *are*, but the fact she's made it her mission to be the first to bed a handsome widower makes me want to hurl. Just as I'm preparing to gather all of my ghostly powers and attack this girl any way I can—shit, I might even be able to throw a knife from that fancy block in her direction if I try hard enough—you kick her out yourself. It's glorious to watch, really, how you tell her with such authority to 'get your shit and get out'. The way her Juvederm-plumped donut lips fall open in shock is one of the favorite things I've witnessed all year.

When she's gone—in a tornado of slamming doors, incensed cursing, and half-donned clothing—you lock the front door behind her, bare-assed, brown-skinned, and Adonis-like in a swatch of moonlight through the foyer window. You break the thick midnight silence with a word: my name.

For a moment I'm weak-kneed, convinced somehow you know I'm here. The prospect frightens me—I've done this detached dance of communication with you for so long—that it feels strange to imagine interacting directly *with* you.

And so I hug the shadows and admire your familiar form, one I used to embrace from behind as you cooked us dinner, or cling to at the airport before you left for another two weeks away from home. I'm no longer able to do either of those things, but I'm still your friendly ghost—your first love, your wife—and one who's determined not to be your last.

Two Years and Eight Months After

"I have a good feeling about this one," I say as you stand before the closet and dress for the evening in a navy-blue suitcoat, slacks, and tan leather lace-ups. It's a getup you wouldn't have been caught *dead* (har, har) wearing when we were married, but you're a fancy executive now, and this girl is special. Your date tonight sort of looks like me, too— shoulder-length, wavy brown hair; petite; attractive in a composed, Type-A kind of way—which I take as a compliment, if a bit masochistic-leaning on your part.

She's another online match, a lawyer who seems too smart for you (although we thought that about me too). Her first message was politc and personalized, asking about your favorite food. You'd actually seemed to heed my suggestions as I told you each night how best to communicate with her during that pivotal introductory period—not too infrequently, not too often, always with proper grammar and punctuation, laying the wit and self-deprecating humor on thick—and you'd arranged a date at an upscale Brazilian steakhouse in downtown by the third day of chatting.

You've got a spring in your step now as you pour some more kibble in the cat's bowl, adding a spritz of cologne to that naked patch of skin above your collarbone I used to nuzzle on sleepy weekend mornings.

"Have fun," I call out in your wake, but you're already through the door—and if I'm not mistaken, you're whistling.

Four Years and Three Months After

The wedding was understated, chic, and an altogether classy affair I would've approved of myself. The reception was nice too, and there was dancing and music and cake-smashing in each other's faces, and you looked so goddamned happy baby, *so* happy, happier than I could remember you looking on *our* wedding day. I cried about that, but only for a little while.

Once you two leave for your honeymoon, I materialize back in the apartment. The cat's at your parents' place for a week, so it's lonely here now; your laugh and her laugh and your shared inside jokes and frequent lovemaking sounds have become a somber kind of music to me, a melancholic soundtrack that hurts to listen to but that I'm still not ready to turn off.

I watch a reality show as a distraction (she likes them too, and records my favorites), but it doesn't diminish the swirling, unsettled sensation where my stomach used to be.

"Is it time?" I say aloud to the silver-haired TV show host on the screen. You're married now, I've been replaced; my plan, for all intents and purposes, is complete. Yet I'm still not ready to go.

I recline on the sofa and ignore the silvery doorway in my periphery, checking every so often to make sure it's still there.

Five Years After

Normally I'd avoid going to another hospital, but today's a special occasion.

Your new wife's a champion, I'll give her that; I never wanted kids and so you said you didn't either, but based on the way you've doted on her for the past nine months, rubbing coconut butter on the stretched skin of her belly while murmuring in baby-speak to the little life growing beneath your hand, I've been convinced otherwise.

When the labor's over and a high-pitched squeal reaches everyone's ears, *your* expression is the one I look at as the baby comes into view—and it answers the question I've been asking since the day I died.

Later in the recovery room, all is quiet and still, the low, beige-pink lighting of the room far less invasive than it was during my visit years back. The baby is at your wife's breast, periodically eating and falling asleep, and your wife's drifting off too. You sit in the rocking chair to their left, studying them with a slight frown.

"It's scary, isn't it," I muse from the other side of your wife's hospital bed. "So much to take care of. So much to protect; that's why I didn't want one."

You wipe some tears from those beautiful brown eyes, and I know what you're thinking.

"Don't do that," I warn, more forcefully than I've spoken to you in a long time. "Stop it *right now*. That day wasn't your fault or mine, and there's nothing you could've done. You can't worry each day you might lose them too, okay? You can't." I round the hospital bed to kneel in front of you, and you stare right through me as usual. "I kept my promise, and now *you* need to keep one—you need to be free, Dan. You need to *live*. Because you've got so much to live for."

You wipe at your cheeks, at the wetness gathering in the patchy dark stubble along your jawline.

You smile.

Five Years and One Day After

She's one cute baby; takes after you the most, I think, but I'm biased. You've always been the best-looking person I've ever met.

The nurses are taken with her, remarking on what a good baby she is, so mild-mannered and sweet and *smiley*. You and your family are all ready to go;

everything's packed, and the baby's received the health check go-ahead to send everyone home.

There's a shimmering doorway here in the hospital too—I've already seen several people go through it during our last two days here. I tried to peek around them to what awaited there, to read by their body language whether it was good or terrible, but I didn't really need to—it leads somewhere nice, and I think I've always known that.

The doctor just said it's time to go. Everyone is ready; the baby's wrapped up tight in a cream-colored onesie, and your wife's all settled in the wheelchair.

"What's her name?" the doctor asks, grinning down at the sleeping baby in the crook of your wife's arm. I expect you to respond the way you have been this entire time—that you both want to spend a few days with her first, to see what feels right.

But you don't say that.

Instead, you say "Eva," and I go rigid where I've been standing in the corner of the room.

"Her name is Eva," you say again, but you're not looking down at the baby, or at the doctor, or at your wife. You're looking at me.

"Eva," the doctor says, surveying your daughter with a smile. "I like that."

Your wife looks a little taken aback, but not for long. "I like it too," she replies, removing one arm from the swaddled baby to reach out and squeeze your hand. She knows who I am, obviously, and as far as I can tell this decision was never settled on—it was always, "Let's just wait and see."

"I've always liked you," I say to your wife as she cradles the baby close, cooing the girl's newly christened name a few times. "Keep taking care of him, okay?"

The doctor leaves, followed by the nurse wheeling your wife and daughter down the hall toward the parking lot. You stay here though, and so do I.

"Goodbye," you whisper, eyes unfocused and roving around the small hospital room. We were in a place like this once, for a much more heartrending reason than this. It's time we were both freed of it.

"Goodbye," I reply, and you dip your chin down, an infinitesimal nod, an acknowledgement. A letting go of that which is already gone.

When you walk out and down the hall the way your family went, I don't follow. Instead, I turn toward the doorway, which grows in size as I approach it, getting brighter around the edges, humming lowly, like the distant crash of waves while napping on the sand in bright sunshine, or that wondrous rumble of imaginary surf accessible at any time if one just cups a seashell to their ear. I grasp the door handle and it's warm in my palm; the first real, identifiable sensation I've had in years.

It feels wonderful.

And I go through.

See Ashley R. Carlson's story "The Friendly Ghost" online at Metaphorosis.
If you liked it, leave a comment. Authors love that!
Remember to subscribe to our e-mail updates so you'll know when new stories are posted."

About the story

The inspiration for my story about a deceased wife who "haunts" her husband and strives to help him discover fulfillment and happiness after her death came from a similar conversation in my own relationship.

My partner also worked far from home at the time, and in a field that had risks. While we didn't talk often about something happening, the danger was there—and one day we discussed our expectations for one another if the other person died. Morbid, I know, but I've always been a bit of a "what if-fer". (Is that a word? I'm going with it.)

This got me thinking about what it would be like to die and watch your spouse move on with their life—to actively participate in it, even, because you love them so much that you want them to fully experience all that life has to offer, even when you're not a part of it.

From there it was just a few days for a first draft, then a couple rounds of revising, sending the story out for beta feedback, more revising based on that feedback, submissions followed by another three rounds of revising, and the finished accepted piece! (The journey of a story from conception to completion requires so many more evolutions and versions than I first expect—and is 10,000 times better for it in the end.)

A question for the author

Q: If you could talk to your novice-writer self, what bit of advice would you give?

A: I would have a hard time whittling down my response to this (there were so many things I was naive about, and still am), but ultimately I would say these things:

1. Don't expect any sort of success or recognition from the first or tenth or twentieth thing you write or publish. This is a marathon, and a really, really slow one. Write because you love it and have a hunger to do it, and for no other reason than this.

2. Don't write typical stuff with typical characters — tropes; gender-conforming; predominantly white; a host of other problems that don't promote diversity. You're going to fall into this trap, and you're going to learn and grow and move away from it, but just be informed and a better promoter of diversity in fiction from the very beginning.

About the author

Ashley is an award-winning author and freelance editor in Phoenix, Arizona. When she's not writing or editing, Ashley enjoys traveling (oftentimes internationally), playing Scrabble with her fiancé (to whom she loses a lot more often than she likes to), and fostering kittens through Arizona Animal Welfare League.

www.ashleyrcarlson.com,

@AshleyRCarlson1

They Build 'Em Tough on Magna Mater

R.W.W. Greene

George's voice crackled over the headset radio. "You going tonight?"

"Not hardly. Pa fined me hard last time. Claimed I forgot to plug Bessie back in and cost us a day's work." Zeke spit a glob of bright orange newbacco juice into a can he'd taped to the inside of the tractor's cockpit. "I plugged her in. Just didn't have time for a full recharge."

"Like your Pa would know anything about a day's work," George said. "He don't remember the last time he done one."

"He weren't always like that." Zeke moved the control sticks in unison, and

Bessie reached out to grasp a four-ton bale of threefalfa in her heavy metal arms. The tractor hefted the bale, servos whining as it moved the load into position and added it to the neat, two-story stack on top of the crawler. "Used to be he worked as hard as anybody."

Zeke's pa hadn't been the same since his wife died of Scylla, a native virus that seemed to take every Terrestrial mammal with two X chromosomes as a personal insult.

The red giant overhead baked the community farmlands, the remnants of a small mountain range pounded into submission from orbit a century before. George's tractor picked up a bale and set it across from Zeke's. They worked with their canopies popped so they could see each other and catch what little breeze there was. "Too bad you ain't going. Got a couple of boys from over the creek looking to brawl. Jake says they got money."

"How much money?"

"Enough to make it interesting."

"Any girls coming?"

"There'll be a few girls along. Whether they've already made their picks," the arms of George's big farm mech dropped its sides with a crash, "you take your chances."

Zeke and Bessie maneuvered another bale to the top of the stack. "Wish I could go."

"Sneak out."

"Bessie ain't what you call 'sneaky.' "

George let his tractor answer for him. The whines, clanks, and hisses blended into the familiar sound of preparations for the long winter ahead. Soon, the stack of bales atop the crawler rose to the tractors' three-story limit.

George swabbed sweat off his face with a red bandanna and squinted at the blue-green sky. "You see Perserpina yet?"

Zeke took a long look. The big moon, Ceres, was almost always in sight, but Perserpina, tiny and erratic, didn't show until she was good and ready—usually long after he was willing to call it a day. "Close enough. Besides, we wait much longer, we'll be travelin' in the dark, and the bunyips will get us."

The yips were much less a problem than they used to be, but they made a good excuse for knocking off work. George and Zeke walked their tractors to the back of the crawler and clomped up the ramp into riding position. The crawler's autopilot blinked awake, and the big vehicle shuddered into unhurried motion.

Zeke propped his feet up on the tractor's control panel and rolled a cigarette. "Is everyone going?"

"Everyone I talked to." George glanced sidelong at his friend. "Pomona might be there."

"What's that s'posed to mean?"

"I know you ain't goin' with her no more, but," George shrugged, "someone will. Probably soon. Might be one of those boys from across the creek."

Calling it a creek would have been laughable on any other planet. It was two miles wide, with class-four rapids along most its length, but it was still a baby compared to most of the rivers and streams on the world.

Zeke scowled. Two months before, he and Pomona had been tight as snicks. He still wasn't sure what had set her off, asking questions about the future, wanting him to buy himself free of his pa, like it were that easy. He hadn't put up much of a fight when she broke it off. "None of my business."

"Hope that makes you feel better when you're pullin' your own pecker in back of your Pa's barn." George had one leg draped over the side of his tractor's cockpit and was sipping something clear from a jar. "Suit yourself. Maybe I'll let you know what happens."

The crawler piloted itself to the co-op silos, and George and Zeke herded their tractors down the exit ramp. The crawler took care of the unloading itself. It would be recharged and ready for work in the morning. George waggled his jar at Zeke. "You come out tonight, you might get some."

Zeke lifted Bessie's arm in a wave. "I go out tonight I might as well not come home."

George turned his tractor toward his small homestead about five miles southwest. Zeke watched until his friend's green-and-yellow mech was nearly out of sight.

He had been trying not to think about Pomona. They'd met in the crèche years ago, when her name had been Paul, but memories of that awkward little boy had long been replaced by the freckled vision that had come back from the mothership with new pronouns and a big smile. They'd hit it off at the Harvest Dance and dated for nearly eight months before she ended it.

None of my business what she does.
Zeke turned Bessie toward home.

Minerva met him at the gate. Zeke lowered the tractor to one knee and glared at the little girl from the cockpit. "Pa catches you outside the fence after dark, you won't sit down for a week."

"Pa's not here." Minerva folded her arms and glared back. "Trudi's in the cistern again."

The latest Scylla vaccine had saved barely fifty percent of Minerva's crèche, but it had proved near a hundred-percent effective on hybrid cows like Trudi.

"Get up here so the bunyips won't get you." Zeke lowered Bessie's hand so Minerva could climb on, and lifted her to the open-air passenger saddle he'd rigged up on the mech's left shoulder. "Weren't you supposed to be watching her?"

"I just looked away for a minute." The girl stomped her foot. "She's stupid."

Or she's tired of you fussing at her. The last time Trudi had ended up in the cistern, Pa had sworn up and down that he'd take her to the slaughterhouse if it ever happened again.

"It's the manatee genes," Minerva said. "Sometimes she forgets she ain't s'posed to like swimming."

Zeke brought Bessie to a halt at the edge of the big water tank.

"There she is!" Minerva stood up in the saddle and pointed. "In the corner."

Sure enough, the cow was neck deep in the cistern, looking like she was about to drop dead from exhaustion.

"You sit back down and put your belt on. I'll get her." Like most of the multi-purpose mechs on Magna Mater, Bessie was roughly human shaped. Two arms, two legs, and a broad torso where the cockpit was. "You belted in?"

"Do I look stupid?" Minerva said.

"Stupid enough to let the cow try to drown itself." Zeke made a tripod of Bessie's knees and her left arm and carefully extended the right into the cistern toward the cow. "Don't worry none, Trudi. This won't hurt a bit." Bessie spread her fingers wide before wrapping them like a steel cage around Trudi's midsection. "Got her!"

Zeke lifted the cow carefully. Trudi only massed a half ton or so, but the position was awkward. He flipped a switch to extend Bessie's outriggers. No sense sending the tractor into the cistern, too. He got the dripping cow to ground level and swung her away from the cistern. Minerva clapped her hands.

Zeke got Bessie back to her feet. "Where do you want her?"

"In her house, silly!"

Zeke walked the tractor toward the house and set the cow down inside the corral he'd set up for her there. He raised Bessie's hand to shoulder level and waited for Minerva to climb on. "You let her get out again, Pa's liable to turn her into dinner."

Minerva stamped her foot. "He will not! She's mine. He gave her to me!"

"Don't put much stock in that, Mini Girl. He'll take her away just as quick." Bessie lowered her hand to the ground, and Minerva stepped off. "But he won't hear it from me. You get inside now. Fence is on, but I reckon you're pretty enough for a bunyip to go to some trouble to eat."

Minerva flashed him a grin and ran to the front door. Zeke turned Bessie toward the barn and triggered open the tall door. Once he was sure the mech was locked down and powered off, Zeke descended the ladder rungs running down her body and plugged her in. He patted her leg. "Good work today, old girl. Few years, I'll have enough saved up so I can buy you out from under Pa, and we'll run off together. Start our own stead." He checked the maintenance board, scowling at a row of yellow telltale lights. "Those leg units are thinking about going again. I told Pa we needed a new set, but …" He shook his head. "I'll climb in there and see what I can do in the morning."

He left the barn and took a look around the family compound. The lights at the top of the old silo were even closer to the ground than yesterday, creeping lower and lower as the structure listed. Pa kept saying he was going to take it down but hadn't gotten around to it. Taken down neat there'd be plenty of salvage, but letting it crash to the ground would likely bust open the shell and ruin the works inside. Zeke continued up the path to the house.

"Where's Pa?" he said, careful not to let the screen door slam behind him.

"Up to the hollow with Uncle Pranav." Tim, the youngest of Zeke's six brothers, was at the kitchen table doing his homework. "Said he won't be back 'til late."

Late morning most likely. Uncle Pranav ran a distillery in the hollow, and Pa went up there a few times a month to "help out". He'd be back close to noon, stinking and aching, his fancy new tractor hauling him home on autopilot.

"Minerva come through here?"

"Went up to her bedroom. She was swearing a streak at that cow of hers. You get her out?"

"Don't tell Pa she fell in again." Zeke took a seat and inspected the auto-cooker in the center of the table. Soup again. "Where are the rest of the young uns?"

"Everyone's inside, Mother. Don't get your skirt in a knot."

Zeke cuffed his brother on the back of his head, barely mussing his hair. "I had a skirt; I'd give it to you. Closest you'll ever get to a girl." He pulled a bowl out of the stack and filled it with the nondescript soup. "What you working on?"

"Calculus. It's pretty easy."

"Never got to it." Zeke spooned soup into his mouth. "Dropped out the year before I would have."

"Why do I have to stay in, then? I hate school."

"I'm the eldest. It's my job to help Pa run the farm," Zeke said. "Your job is to get good grades and do something better with your life. Be a freighter captain, maybe. Or a doctor."

"What if I want to be a farmer?"

"It's hard work, little man. And tractors don't come cheap."

"I can do it!"

"You can, but you don't have to. Get your learnin' in and move to the city." Zeke shoved his bowl into the recycler and stood up. "I'm going up to bed."

Zeke showered, then climbed the narrow stairs to the second floor and the ladder that led to his little room in the attic. Age had its privileges. He and Minerva were the only ones besides Pa with private rooms. Zeke crawled onto his mattress and stared at the bare beams a few feet above his face. Tim was eleven. Minerva would be seven in the fall. In another eight or nine years she'd start getting marriage proposals and offers for eggs. It would be up to Pa to negotiate a price, with a healthy cut for himself, of course, but the final decision would be hers. She could ignore the whole thing, marry for love, or never marry at all, but the money was always a temptation, and Pa would surely pressure her. Pomona would probably be hitching up soon, too.

No sense sticking around, with her options.

He put his hands behind his head. No wonder Pa drank so much.

Zeke's wristcuff buzzed, and he pulled his arm free so he could see it. It was George. Zeke poked the screen to answer the call. George's face was sweaty and excited. "You got to get out here! There's a Vidcom crew here filming. *Mech Mayhem.* They've got a half million to split among the top three fighters."

"You're funnin' me." Zeke's heart raced. Vidcom was the most popular network in the system and had money to burn. They liked to film the mech brawls, but they'd never been as far out as Magna Mater.

"Like hell I am." The image on Zeke's wristcuff spun as George moved to show the Vidcom camera crew setting up. A tall blonde man in the latest system fashion was directing them. "They've got a brand-new brawler mech here taking on all comers. They're giving a thousand just for agreeing to fight it on camera, plus first, second, third prizes. Get out here!"

"Shit!" A thousand credits wasn't enough to matter much, but even a third-place finish might give him enough to buy Bessie out from under his Pa and claim his own stead. Zeke slid out of bed and put his work clothes back on.

"Make sure Minerva stays inside," he told Tim as he passed by. "I'll be back late."

"Where you going?" the boy said.

Zeke closed the front door on the question and hurried to the barn, glancing left and right. The fence was usually enough to keep the bunyips out of the compound, but sometimes one slipped through and spent the night prowling outside the buildings. The really big ones had all been killed off years before, but the leftovers were fast and angry, more than enough to take down an unarmed man.

He entered the barn through the side door and flipped the switch that turned on the light. "We got a chance to make some money, old girl." He punched the wake-up command into the maintenance board. Bessie was only up to a half charge, but it would do for a few fights and the jog to the ring. Zeke climbed up the ladder to the cockpit and strapped in. "This could be it."

The old tractor responded to Zeke's commands and clomped through the big door. Zeke sent a coded message to the

NavNet and got a ping back with the current location of the brawl. Mech fighting wasn't illegal—not much was on Magna Mater—but it was dangerous and potentially expensive. The Homestead Council zoomed in to break things up anytime they could figure out where the brawl was, so the boys who put it on kept moving it. Bessie's navscreen lit up with a location about two miles away at a nice, easy power-saving jog.

"Let's go, girl." Bessie lurched forward.

The off-world brawler mech looked smooth and alien among the local jalopies and tractors standing around it. "The hell is *that* thing?" Zeke said once he'd reached the ground and entered the pool of spectators.

George handed Zeke his jar. "They call it Galaxy Chrome. Latest model. Looking to make a name by taking on the local talent."

"Sheeit!" Zeke studied the sleek, shiny mech. "None of us have the money for something like that!"

George collected the jar back and took a long swallow. "They're not looking to sell to us. If it looks good kicking some hicks around, all the central-system rich kids will want one."

The brawler mech was at least four feet taller than anything the locals had.

"You going to fight it?" Zeke said.

"Was until I saw it. A thousand wouldn't cover the repairs I'd have to make, and I'd probably have to rent a tractor to finish out the season. The winter would be mighty lean."

"But what if you won?"

George patted his mech's green leg. "That thing could put a hole right through my cockpit and wave at everybody on the other side."

"Guess nothing runs away like a Deere."

George snorted. "Ain't runnin', but I ain't stupid, either."

"Anyone else try?"

"Tom Riley. Lasted about two minutes. Thing picked his jalopy right off the ground and tossed it twenty feet." He pointed. "He's over there in the first-aid tent. He was thrown out of the cockpit."

"Tom's mech ain't much better than a lawn mower. He shouldn'ta tried."

"You be sure to tell him that when he wakes up."

A thin man in a powder-blue jumpsuit climbed up the fancy mech and stood in its passenger saddle. He fiddled with something on his wristcuff, and his voice boomed out of the mech's speakers. "Who's next?" He looked around at the local brawlers. Most of their mechs had come straight from the fields, but a few of the better-off had built ones just for fighting.

"I'm in." A tall mech lurched forward. Aamil Baig's jalopy had started life as a firebot. It was still bright red in places, and Aamil ran the siren and flashing lights as he stepped into the ring. His mech had the longest reach of any in the settlement, and a secret weapon, but it was painfully slow. "But only if you raise it to five thousand."

The slicker shrugged. "Done."

"Start your cameras." Aamil closed his mech's cockpit and turned on its lights. The siren whooped as the slicker climbed down and shouted instructions to his camera crew.

Galaxy Chrome moved like its joints were made of oil and marched to a spot about fifty feet away where it waited for Aamil and his mech. The slicker walked between them and signaled for Aamil to cut the lights and siren. He looked at one of his camera bots and flashed a confident grin. "Fellow sentients, have we got a fight for you!"

Zeke tuned into the feed in time to hear the *Mech Mayhem* score swell.

The slicker grinned again. He was better looking on the feed than he was in person. "Magna Mater. The wildest planet the system has to offer. The land is hard, and it's eager," the slicker narrowed his eyes, "to kill."

The feed switched to a recording of a bunyip swarm. The big reptiles thundered by the camera until one, probably baited by the operator, turned and roared directly into the lens.

"The natives have to fight every day just to survive. They're tough, and their mechs are tougher." He flung his arm up. "But are they tough enough to handle Galaxy Chrome?" The feed switched to show a close up of the big mech's cockpit. "The newest mech from BrawlerBot, Inc.? Let's find out!"

The feed switched back to the slicker's face, and he grinned right on cue. "You boys ready?"

Half the screen filled with Aamil's bearded face, the other with the bland good looks of Galaxy Chrome's pilot. Aamil nodded and the other pilot lifted his hands from his controls to offer a double thumbs up.

"Then let's get ready to ruuuuuuuumble!" The slicker ran straight ahead to get out of the battle zone. Aamil turned the sirens and lights back on and moved his mech's left foot ahead for balance.

Galaxy Chrome bent low and charged straight at Aamil.

Zeke grinned. The off-worlder was playing right into Aamil's game. The bearded miner knew his mech was slow and usually waited for the other fighter to make the first move. The jalopy crouched and raised its arms to meet the charge. Chrome closed the distance fast, the ground shuddering with every running step.

Zeke knew the move Aamil was about to make; most of the brawlers on Magna Mater did, but there was no way the off-worlder would. This was going to be good.

The rockets mounted on the fire mech's wrists roared into life, and its big red fists shot forward ... and kept going, trailing steel cables. The arms on Aamil's mech could extend seventy yards in less than two seconds, part of its rapid-rescue package. Aamil called it his "Telescope Punch," and it was usually enough to take out an unwary opponent. It had to be, because it took Aamil two minutes to reel the arms back in and get the fists back into place.

Galaxy Chrome pivoted on one foot—it moved so fast Zeke wasn't exactly sure what happened. Both the red fists missed their marks and shot to the ends of their cables before thumping to the ground. The off-world mech took two more steps, grabbed the cables, and ripped them out, leaving Aamil with sparking stumps.

The *Mech Mayhem* score swelled, and Zeke's vidscreen showed the move again in slow motion. "Who's next?" the slicker howled.

Five-thousand, about enough for a beater mech, was the magic number for the boys with custom-made brawlers. The Lajoie twins stepped up. They piloted their jalopy, a souped-up construction machine, as a duo. Galaxy Chrome ripped it right in half, spilling the Lajoies to the ground in a shower of sparks and jagged metal. If he was lucky, Trevor Lajoie would keep his right arm.

The brawl continued and broken mechs piled up on the sides of the field. The slicker threw his arms in the air as Galaxy Chrome's latest victim was hauled away. "Who's next?"

"You gotta fight him," George said. "You're the only one who stands a chance."

Zeke shook his head. "Not even. You saw what he did to the twins!"

"You're better than they are!" George said. "You're better than all of us."

"Not good enough," Zeke said. "That thing's taken out seven brawlers without getting a scratch."

"We're raising the ante," the slicker announced. "Ten thousand just for stepping in the ring with the mighty Galaxy Chrome!"

George swore. "They must be taking orders for those things right and left."

Zeke's head swam. Ten thousand was a lot of money. Half again what it would cost to buy Bessie away from Pa. Enough to file for a small stead. He raised his hand. "I'm in. We'll fight."

Zeke unplugged Bessie from the network's big generator. The forced charge wasn't good for the tractor's batteries, but he needed them as close to full as possible to have any hope of keeping up with Galaxy Chrome. The slicker put his hand on Zeke's back. "You ready?"

"If the money's still good."

"The money's fine. We'll drop it into your account soon as the cameras start rolling. Win or lose."

"Make sure to keep the prize money ready, too. I'm taking your pretty bot down," Zeke said. "You ready, girl?"

Bessie couldn't answer, but it seemed like she moved a little quicker whenever she was in the ring, responded better to the controls. Like she enjoyed fighting.

The slicker stepped between the two mechs and raised his arms in the air. "Sentients, I am proud to present the next fight of the night. The mighty Galaxy Chrome and, fighting for the honor of Magna Mater, Zeke Liu and his Battlin' Bessie!"

VidCom graphic enhancements made it seem like an audience of thousands surrounded the ring, baying for blood and twisted metal. In reality, a few dozen farmers, miners, and builders yelled themselves hoarse and made as much noise as they could.

Bessie pounded the hammer side of her right fist into the cup of her palm, banging her own war drum. The local mechs left standing picked up the beat, and the field echoed with the clash of steel on hardened steel.

The slicker signaled for silence, and the beat tapered off. "You boys ready?"

Zeke nodded, knowing his face would be on millions of screens around the system. The pilot of the off-world mech shrugged and pretended to yawn.

The comm unit in Bessie's cockpit stuttered to life. "Zeke!" Tim hollered through it. "Minerva's outside the fence! She's gone after that fool cow again!"

On the opposite side of the control panel a red light started flashing, and a siren howled. A bunyip-swarm alert. Everyone in town would be getting the same signal and securing their steads in response.

"Let's get ready to—!" the slicker began.

"What do you want me to do?" Tim sounded breathless.

"Shit!" Zeke put Bessie in motion, using the newly charged battery to bring her up to speed. The entire VidCom audience, millions of sentients on dozens of planets, watched him flee the ring. "I'm on my way!"

Zeke jumped Bessie over a ravine. "You stay put and keep the other young uns inside," he told Tim via the comm. The mech's worn leg servos sent her telltales flickering into the red zone as she landed on the other side. "I'm going to find our little sister and skin her alive."

If the bunyips don't beat me to it. Minerva had barely been walking the last time the monsters went on the move. Three or four times in a generation the yips spawned, moving across the land to a new river or stream, killing and eating everything in their path. Smart people got out of their way. NavNet was predicting the swarm would be going through the biggest cluster of steads, right past the one claimed by Zeke's Pa.

Zeke pushed Bessie to run faster and powered up her leg extenders to gain a few extra meters with each stride. The warning lights for her leg servos went further into the red, a harbinger of failure, but the mech ate up the distance faster.

Zeke heard the bunyips before he saw them: a slithery mass of low growls, angry roars, and heavy footfalls. He activated Bessie's vision enhancements and zoomed in on the swarm. He'd never seen so many of the things. Little ones just a little bigger than a standing man and others that stood taller at the shoulder than Bessie did. Zeke's headset radio crackled.

"I thought we'd killed off all the big uns," George said.

Zeke craned his neck to see George's tractor jog up behind him.

"That's a lot of lizards," George said. "Let's get to high ground and wait it out."

"Can't. Minerva's out here somewhere. She ran out after that cow of hers."

George cursed. "That ain't good. Both likely to end up yip shit."

Zeke cranked up the magnification and scanned the grounds of the stead for any sign of his sister.

"I see her," George said. He pointed with his mech's hand. Minerva had climbed to the top of the old silo and was hanging on for dear life a couple of meters above the reach of the tallest bunyip. "She's safe."

"No, she's not," Zeke said. "That silo would fall over if the wind blew hard. It will come right down if one of those big bastards bumps up against it."

A new voice cut into their conversation. "I'll get her."

Galaxy Chrome darted out in front of them and ran into the swarm, trailed by a flock of camera drones.

"Sentients," the slicker chortled over the VidCom feed. "This is unprecedented. BrawlerBot's latest masterpiece is taking on an entire flock of the most dangerous creatures in the system, and you're seeing it here, live!"

"That ain't a good idea," George said. "One or two of them is about all ..."

Galaxy Chrome's pilot yelled in fear as the gleaming mech became a target of several of the smaller bunyips. They swarmed up the mech's legs to the cockpit and began raking it with their claws. The pilot made the mistake of trying to take a long step out of the scrum, and the bunyips' weight made the big mech topple to the ground with a crash.

"Well, that done it," George said.

One of Galaxy Chrome's thrashing legs grazed the silo, and Minerva's precarious perch tilted closer to the feeding frenzy below.

"Get up! Get up!" the slicker yelled over the VidCom feed.

The feed from Galaxy Chrome crackled. "There're too many of them! I can't get loose!"

The big mech's thrashing was attracting the attention of some of the bigger bunyips. It would take time, but they could crack the brawler mech's cockpit like an egg.

"Hold still!" Zeke said. "I'm coming in!"

"That ain't smart," George said.

"No choice." Zeke made sure his canopy was locked tight, and jogged to the edge of the swarm. He'd taken Bessie through rapids and rock falls before, and figured a shuffle step was the best approach. He moved the tractor forward slowly, barely lifting her feet.

"They're coming at you!" George said.

Zeke caught the first bunyip in mid leap and tossed it back toward his friend. "Make yourself useful and step on it."

The second bunyip hit Bessie in the back and stuck, clawing for the soft meat inside. Zeke shuffled faster, punching away the yips he could catch and ignoring the ones he couldn't. A mid-sized bunyip hit Bessie behind her knees and nearly bowled her over.

"Watch it!" George said.

Zeke didn't have the breath to respond. He moved without thinking, dodging with as much flexibility as Bessie allowed and putting her hardened fists into the heads and torsos of any bunyip he could see. He made it into the shadow of the silo and craned his neck to look up. Minerva's face was tear-streaked, but she looked more angry than afraid. Her knuckles, where she clutched the railing, were white. He switched on Bessie's loud speakers. "I'm right under you, Mini."

"They killed Trudi!" she said. "Ripped her all to pieces!"

The anguish in her voice made him ache. He would have done anything to keep her from having to see that. "You hold on!" Zeke considered his options. He could use Bessie to brace the silo and hope he could hold it long enough for the swarm to pass or... "George, I'm going to need you to come in here."

"The hell I will!" George said.

"I gotta get her down from there, George!"

George swore softly but repetitively as he shuffled his tractor into the swarm. He played it safer than Zeke had, but he was at his friend's side in minutes. "Now what?"

"Just keep them off me." Zeke dropped Bessie's outriggers and extended her legs to their full height. He got an extra three meters out of it, putting himself just under Minerva's perch. He opened the canopy in time to feel Bessie nearly fall out from under him as she shook under a sharp impact. "George!"

"Sorry about that. One of the middling ones got by. Hurry it up. There's a lot more coming."

Zeke unfastened his safety harness and stood in the seat to grab Minerva under her arms. The passenger saddle didn't offer any protection, so he swung her into the cockpit with him and sealed it back up. "Squeeze behind the seat and stay there. We're not out of this yet." He refastened his harness as Bessie rocked again.

"Hurry, Zeke!" George said. "I'm not funnin' you."

Zeke retracted the outriggers and returned Bessie's legs to normal, bringing the cockpit back in range of the scaly swirl below. "Let's see what we can do for Chrome before we get clear."

He led the way, pushing against the bunyips until he got to the frenzied pile that covered the off-world mech. He grabbed a double handful of bunyips and tossed them aside. George joined him, and, when they got Galaxy Chrome clear enough to see, they grabbed its arms and pulled it to its feet. "Let's go," Zeke said. "Shuffle until you get to the edge of the swarm." He glanced over his shoulder at his sister. "You okay back there?"

"I need to pee," she said.

"You'll wait on that if you know what's good for you. You pee in here, and I'll put you right back up in that silo."

He shuffled Bessie after George's tractor and Galaxy Chrome. Bunyip swarms were single-minded, moving from waterway to waterway over whatever land stood in the way. Funny, they were never as thick in the mountains as they were over the land the colonists had terraformed. Once the mechs were out of its path, they would be largely out of danger. Galaxy Chrome got to the edge of the swarm first and sprinted to a safe distance. The big mech was a mess, its hull battered and dented, shiny finish dulled and gouged by the bunyips' claws, pieces of its decorative superstructure torn away and left behind.

"Look—!" George's warning ended in a blast of static as his green-and-yellow mech tumbled sideways into the swarm. The biggest bunyip Zeke had ever seen roared and gave chase, knocking smaller yips aside like puppies.

"George!" Zeke turned Bessie around and pushed back into the swarm in pursuit of the giant bunyip. The others had cleared off, letting the big yip claim its prey. One of the green tractor's arms had come away in the tumble, and its left leg was twisted underneath it.

"Git outta here, Zeke!" George broadcast. "It's no good both of us getting' kilt."

Bessie muckled on to the big yip's tail with both hands, halting its teeth and claws meters away from the damaged tractor. The bunyip dug in its claws and lunged forward. Zeke extended Bessie's outriggers again and held on, trying to ignore the flashing red lights warning of leg-servo failure.

The yip turned to get his teeth around for an attack on Bessie's hands and legs, but its spine wasn't flexible enough. Bessie hauled up, extending her arms and lifting the yip's hindquarters off the ground by its tail. The scaly creature whipped its head wildly, snapping at anything it could reach. Bessie shuddered and pitched with every shift in weight.

"What's happening?" Minerva said.

"You just hang on, Mini Girl." Zeke gritted his teeth and fought to keep Bessie upright. If she toppled, if the leg servos failed, the bunyip would be on him in seconds, and he had no illusions how the test of claws and teeth versus the old mech's hull would go. If he had a hand free, he could put a hardened fist right through the yip's skull, but he didn't dare let go of the tail for even a second.

An alarm squalled as the leg-servo warning lights went solid red. Bessie's left leg buckled, and she started to topple. Zeke fought to keep her up by hopping on the right leg, but the mech wasn't built for it, and the weight of the bunyip pulled it to the ground. Zeke's teeth came together hard at the impact, and he tasted blood. Minerva screamed. He reached into the seat pocket for his sidearm, but the little gun would be of little use against an enraged yip. Minerva might go unnoticed behind the seat, her scent hidden by the odor of his own spilled blood. He flicked off the gun's safety. The big yip charged. "You son of a bitch!" he said.

Its teeth were a foot away from the cockpit window when a steel fist struck, crashing into the top of the yip's skull and driving its bottom jaw into the dirt. Galaxy Chrome pulled its fist out of the bunyip's cranium and grabbed Bessie by the leg. He hauled her over to George's wreck and grabbed it by the shoulder. Then, step by shuffling step, Galaxy Chrome pulled both tractors to safety in front of the largest viewing audience in Vidcom history.

It took another four hours for the swarm to pass. George shared his jar of hooch with the off-worlder while they watched. Zeke waved the jar away, more concerned with getting Minerva to stop fussing about Trudi.

"I'm gonna kill all of them," she said. Her face was streaked with tears, tiny fists balled up like rocks.

"Hush, Mini," Zeke said. "Leave them be, they'll leave you be. Trudi was just too dumb for her own good." *And too tasty.* Maybe breeding cows wasn't such a good idea. The yips had no interest at all in threefalfa.

Later, neighbors helped him move Bessie to her maintenance cradle in the barn and gave George and his wreck a ride home. The check Vidcom gave George for rights to the video and a personal endorsement of BrawlerBot's new mech put a grin on George's face that lasted all the way to his pillow, which he shared that night with Brian Lance, Galaxy Chrome's handsome pilot.

Zeke tucked Minerva in, commiserated with her some about the cow, and went out to the barn to see Bessie. She had several more gouges and dents, some deep scratches, but she'd already carried a fair share of them. Her frame looked okay in spite of the hard fall. Zeke winced when he ran a diagnostic on her legs. Most everything in there was going to need an overhaul before she could work again, and he'd taken months off her batteries' life with that forced charge.

He was going to catch hell from his pa. Sober, Pa would rage. Drunk, he'd rage and maybe throw hands. Later, he'd cool down some and bill Zeke for the cost of the repairs and ask the Steader's Union to levy a fine. It would wipe out everything Zeke had saved and then some.

Or it would have.

Zeke used his wristcuff to check his new bank balance. His own check from

Vidcom had given him enough in one haul to fix Bessie up, buy her out from under his pa, pay his fine, and set up a nice little stead of his own.

In a season or two, he could petition the Union for custody of the young uns, give them a better living environment and maybe a few more life options. Hell, he might even give Pomona a call and ask her if she'd seen him on Vidcom. He had some answers to her questions about the future now.

In the testimonial the slicker had recorded, both Zeke and George had gassed on and on about how great the off-world mech was, how rugged and fast. Zeke, at least, had been lying through his teeth. He wouldn't take one of the new bots if they offered it to him for free.

He looked up and down Bessie again, older than him by at least twenty years and not a shiny spot in sight. He patted the big mech's leg.

"They can do what they want with the video," he said, "but we both know who the toughest mech in the system is, girl."

Bessie didn't answer—she never did—but he heard her loud and clear. They built 'em tough on Magna Mater.

See R.W.W. Greene's story "They Build 'Em Tough on Magna Mater" online at Metaphorosis. If you liked it, leave a comment. Authors love that!
Remember to subscribe to our e-mail updates so you'll know when new stories are posted.

About the story

I guess this story has its origins in the Kevin Bacon movie "Footloose". There's an awesome/ridiculous scene wherein Ren (Kevin Bacon) and the Jerk Guy are playing chicken on tractors. I won't tell you how the tractor duel came out, but I took this scene into the context of my own semi-rural upbringing and came up with the ideas of bored farm boys drinking 'shine and brawling with their mechs on the weekend. (It's not too far from reality. Most of us were scarred from running dirt bikes into electric fences or flipping over on three-wheelers out in someone's back forty.)

The rest of the story lined up from there. Family obligations and the difficulties inherent in building a new home from scratch. I have this idea that the entertainment on any colony mission would trend heavily into frontier dramas — "Little House on the Prairie", "Jeremiah Johnson", etc. — to get the travelers into the pioneer headspace. Otherwise, I'd think it would be mighty hard to get folks to leave the comforts of their generation ships.

And who knows what waits in the rivers and streams of those new worlds? It would be a massive struggle at first, false steps, new plans, experiments...

I do wonder sometimes if we're still capable of making the leap or if we've gotten way too soft.

A question for the author

Q: What do you think is the single most important quality for a good writer to possess?

A: A small, hard ego. Nothing big and puffed up. Nothing easily punctured. But a tiny kernel of confidence that can weather rejections and distractions and failure and keep them in the chair day after day pounding on the page.

About the author

R.W.W. Greene is a New Hampshire, USA writer. His critically acclaimed, novel-length debut, *The Light Years* sprang forth from Angry Robot Books in February 2020.

rwwgreene.com, @rwwgreene

Shards

Jordan Chase-Young

Shona's seaweed harness creaked loudly as a cold, whistling gale tried to fling her off the Spire. She held onto the masonry until the air stilled, until her guts ceased to cartwheel. In the six years since Shona had escaped the deluge, she'd rarely felt vertigo. Even when her fellow earthmasons raised the Spire as high as it hung now—a mile or so above the ocean that now wrapped the world—the sun-pummeled water below seemed little more than a great sweep of stone she could stand upon if she wanted to.

But thick grey clouds had rolled out of the north that morning, bringing an unpleasant depth to the world. Whenever the wind picked up, she tried not to think of her harness snapping. Tried not to see herself falling, and the Spire—her home, her family—dwindling to a dust-speck in the infinite emptiness above her.

"Everything all right down there?" Hendrick called from the lookout. He was peering over the crenellations four stories up, his cloud of thick red hair bright against bronzed skin. She gave a sign of assurance. "Okay. But I'll pull you up, if this wind gets any worse. Fix what you can in the meantime, my love."

The braids of dried seaweed joining Shona's harness to the lookout quivered as Hendrick retightened them to their iron moorings.

Fix what I can. Hendrick's voice, hard and certain as stone, always centered her. Even when he expected the impossible. *Not even the Allcreator could fix what we broke, my mountain.*

She did her duty anyway, pressing her ear to the cold granite and rapping her knuckles upon it, listening for the chime of ice crystals trapped within.

Like all earthmasons, she could feel the stone as though it were a part of her. Move it like a soft, supple clay with her will. She could sense the cracks the ice had formed: tiny, fine webs of them through the stone. With concentration, Shona knitted these shut beneath her fingers, teasing the ice inside them toward the surface for the sky to reclaim.

Once she'd cleared all the granite she could reach, she shook the rightmost tether to signal for Hendrick to lower her a little, and continued working.

The Spire would not last more than a few years longer. Four, if they were lucky. In the pre-flood days, a good repointing job could have added decades of life to an edifice, if not more, but the earthmasons back then did not have to contend with the endless frost-weathering wrought by a dead world's cruel winds. A great earthmason could have trawled the ocean for replacement minerals, perhaps, but none of the thirty earthmasons to survive the flood had such talent. Not even Archmason Tybalt. The fifty-two lackblooms were even more useless, lacking power over stone.

The Spirefolk must find land, and soon, she thought as Hendrick pulled her back up. *Or our fates will join those of the uncountable multitudes that drowned.*

"That bad?" Hendrick asked, once she was back on the lookout.

He helped her unclasp the harness. She enjoyed the feel of coming out of it, letting the coarse, smelly seaweed plop onto the cold stone floor.

"It could be worse." She kissed his dark lips, rough and dry as barnacles. "We'll have to search harder."

"Six years of this shit." Hendrick looked at the shattered moon half-visible above, no grander than a clod of pumice crushed and strewn in a lazy arc. "If there were land, hummingbird, don't you think we'd have found it by now?"

His honesty always stung, no matter how much she depended on it. "Any earthmasons who could break the moon could survive what comes after. They're out there, my mountain. We will find them."

What would happen after, Shona could not guess. *Let tomorrow deal with tomorrow.*

As she descended the staircase that corkscrewed around the Spire, Shona sighted movement through one of the tall, unglazed windows that marked each landing. It startled her. But she reasoned it must have been a kestrel—one of the Spire's many stowaways—plunging to the sea for an afternoon meal. Her weariness made her jumpier than usual.

In the dungeon, the lowest level of the Spire, nine earthmasons sat shut-eyed in a circle. A few feet above them hovered a ball of dark polished iron: a helmstone, to keep them fixed on a single point of the building's mass. It helped them carry the Spire as one, draw it across the sky with their collective will.

Most days, a meditation circle held seven or eight earthmasons. But today Shona's five-year-old daughter Micah made the ninth. Bronzed and skinny, with the same red whorl of hair as Hendrick, she was sitting in dutiful silence with her legs crossed, her breathing steady.

Eight earthmasons had been lost in the six years since the deluge. Sickness had taken three. Suicide, two others. One earthmason had died from old age. And the last two—the last two had been slain during the Incident, but Shona did not like to think about that.

Micah's eyes shifted behind their lids as Shona padded down the hall beside the meditation circle. *Unfocused.* She was no more ready than Shona would have been at her age. But they did not have the luxury of waiting.

Archmason Tybalt was studying the drylocks in the storage chamber when Shona entered. He gestured with his scruffy chin for her to shut the pinewood door, then went back to scratching figures on a clay slate with his stylus. His grey cat Despond sluiced in and out of his path as he traipsed through the oil-lit gloom, as if afraid to leave Tybalt's shadow.

Shona sensed that something was wrong. She flattened down her work-smock. "Archmason."

"The repointing went well, I trust."

She sighed. No point mincing words. "The walls are weakening faster than I'd thought."

A vein in his bald head moved, like a worm beneath vellum, but his face remained expressionless. "I see. Anything else?"

His hard blue eyes had not faded a bit since his time as a foreman for the Guild of Architects—a hundred lifetimes ago, it must have been. He'd been softer in those days. Gentler. And she'd been elated to join his building team, as any earthmason would have been. But the end of the world had dried out his soul like everyone else's, leaving a husk of duties, procedures, routines. She missed the old Archmason.

"No. Nothing else. But I sense there is something you wish to tell me."

Tybalt's tone was grave. "Someone has been stealing from the drylocks."

She frowned, not quite believing it. "Are you sure?"

"I have counted the figures three times. The papaya and blackcurrant leaves seem untouched. But the figs, carobs, runner beans—all have dwindled much quicker than usual this month." Removing a sharkskin glove, he reached through the iron valve of a drylock, willing the metal around his flesh, and pulled out a few dried runner beans. This made the pendulum scale under the squat, rectangular storage device tick down half a notch. "It is hardly inexplicable. Think how many drowned kingdoms each of these is worth."

"I promise you, I had nothing to do with it."

"Of course not. Do you think I would have made you my successor if I could not trust you? But an earthmason is to blame. And there are only thirty of us, Shona."

Did he have Hendrick in mind? Or Micah? She bristled to think he would ever suspect her family of thievery. *Murder,* in fact, since every soul in the Spire needed fruits and vegetables to keep the Slow Death at bay.

"Whoever it is, we will find them. There are only so many hiding places."

"We will," Tybalt agreed, returning the runner beans to the drylock. "But think what this will do to our relations with the lackblooms. To the threads of trust we've been weaving so carefully these six long years."

"We cannot tell them. Not unless we want to risk another Incident."

"Then how do you propose we catch the thief?"

"I don't know," she said, sadly. "I need time to think about it."

The sun burned red that evening, its reflection on the sea like molten slag pouring from a crucible. The redness spilled through the windows along the stairway, engulfing Shona as she climbed to the feast room, eager for the fish that would soon be served. Shards of moon twinkled in the sky like early stars.

Which earthmason could have stolen the food? Jerold the Younger, who had once served the crownlaws? Reyna, when she wasn't leading a meditation circle? Gellard Grey-Eyes?

Absurd. They were honorable men and women, all of them.

Maybe one of the lackblooms had learned how to bypass the drylocks. But it was her distaste for lackblooms, an ugly relic of the pre-flood world, more than any sort of logic that lent this possibility its appeal. The lackblooms had ruled over the earthmasons for centuries on the strength of their numbers, and had done so with a cruelty matched only by the earthmasons themselves, in the long-ago days when *they* had ruled. The days of the Stone Empire, and the Diamantine Queens, and the Long War that had ended it all.

She couldn't let her anger cloud her judgment. The Incident had taught her the danger of that. Both peoples had slaked their anger with blood that day, a mere fortnight after escaping the deluge. The lackblooms had set it off; she would not forget that. Had threatened to disrupt a meditation circle unless their demands were met. But the earthmasons had been too quick to reply with violence. In the end, it had taken four deaths and far more injuries to convince the Spirefolk that cooperation was the only way.

The two peoples would never love each other—that much Shona knew—but they had reached a peace over the years. Had even worked out their share of duties, the lackblooms fishing and cooking, mending clothes and scrubbing floors, while the earthmasons held up the Spire. It was a brittle contract, held together by habit, but it worked. The thief was a threat to that, and had to be stopped.

"I'm telling you I saw it," Old Lorrick mumbled through a mouthful of fish. "Wings this long"—lifting his arms for the other lackblooms huddled around him, rapt as children—"and wild fierce by the look of it. Weren't no bird neither, I can swear to that. Not like any bird I seen in my life."

"Sounds like you've been in the sun too much," Hendrick shot from his corner of the feast room, with a chortle that sent bits of chewed fish flying.

"Hendrick," Shona cautioned. She was cutting Micah's blubber into edible chunks, her knife honed to razor-sharpness for the task.

Old Lorrick waved off Hendrick's remark with theatric weariness.

"When did you see this creature?" Shona asked.

Old Lorrick itched his scraggly beard. "Two, three hours ago, while I was fixing up the seine. It was green, it was. Not like emerald but sort of like that. Darker."

The highborn known as Cadmus, who resembled a great bat in his overlarge cloak, ceased stirring his blackcurrant tea and looked up, his dour smooth-shaven face suddenly bright with interest. The lackblooms had named Cadmus their leader not long after the deluge, just as the earthmasons had named Tybalt theirs —but Cadmus' authority had been eclipsed over the years by the Archmason's, as anyone could have predicted; a lackbloom's ancestry counted for little on the Spire, while an earthmason's talent counted for everything. With no small bitterness, Cadmus and his closest friends had come to accept that fact, so long as the earthmasons still called him "liege" and treated him as such.

"Like jade?" Cadmus asked.

"That's it," said Old Lorrick. "Like jade. But in spite of its flying, I'd swear it was featherless as a snake. Made me think dragons. Like what traders used to sight sometimes over the northern parts, beyond the reach of love or law."

One by one, the other sixty Spirefolk in the feast room began to take interest.

Cadmus sipped his tea. "I've never known you to lie, Lorrick. I believe you saw this thing."

Hendrick gave a snort.

"Is there something you wish to tell me, blacksmith?"

"Yes, my liege. I think your cloak's too tight if you credit this old fisherman's visions."

Several lackblooms scowled at his disrespect.

"Well, unlike you, I can read," said Cadmus. "And I have read *Stories of the Ice Seas*. It is always the same tale, of traders espying dragons made of gold or jade. Some say they are small gods that brought the powers of the earthmasons into the world. But I think they are beasts that earthmasons fashioned during the Stone Empire and loosed upon their foes, in the days before we cleanfolk took over and made things right. Now they wander the skies without purpose, aimless and alone."

Steg the Spearmaker, a tiny grizzled otter of a man in a filthy work-smock, huffed at this. "Mudrats ain't gods, Cadmus—making things that can live after 'em like that."

His slur inspired a ripple of insults from the earthmasons, which he just laughed off.

"That's enough of that," said Shona, stifling a childish image of Hendrick cleaning the smile off Steg's face. "I thought I saw something in the sky this evening as well, but I did not get a good look at it. I assumed it was one of our kestrels. Could that be what you saw, Lorrick? A kestrel, and a trick of the light?"

Old Lorrick shook his thin grey head. "I know what I seen, stonemover. And that was not it."

That night, in their family chamber, Shona and Hendrick and Micah washed their faces and arms with warm water from the furnace, changed into their bed-smocks, and prayed at each of their four small shrines to the Facets of the Allcreator.

Years ago, sleep would have sliced through Shona's consciousness like a headsman's axe the moment she laid down. But she didn't fall into that pleasant blackness right away anymore, even with Hendrick's comforting arm slung over her. Worries and aches kept her gazing at the wall long after she'd turned out the oil lamps. Gazing and wondering why she still prayed to a god she no longer believed in, not truly.

"Tense as stone, you are," Hendrick whispered. "What's wrong?"

She checked that the door was shut, afraid her voice might carry into Micah's room. Then she told him about the stolen rations, feeling his pulse rise in his closely pressed chest.

"Whoever it was, I'll throw 'em in the fucking sea. But how'd they get into the storage room? It's damned impossible to break in without the meditation circle noticing. Unless—"

"They break in from the outside."

"That'd leave traces in the masonry, wouldn't it?"

"I hadn't thought of that. Yes, it would."

"Have you noticed anything odd? When you're closing up the cracks?"

Shona thought about it. "I haven't worked on that part of the Spire in months. By Tybalt's reckoning, the thief hasn't been at it that long." She was seized by an impulse. "I can look now. If you'll help."

"It's the dead of night, Shona. You're to lead the meditation circle tomorrow morning. Besides, Tybalt's got the key and he's asleep."

"We don't need to go through the storage room."

The lookout was dark and empty. Nights were much darker now that the moon was just a thin sneer of shards between the stars. Cold wind whipped Shona's face raw as Hendrick fastened a pair of oil lamps to her harness. She kissed him, grateful he'd agreed to this despite his reluctance.

"Be quick about it," he said. "Two minutes. Alright? I don't want to have to explain this if we're noticed."

"I will, my mountain. I promise."

He loosened the moorings, a little at a time, as Shona climbed over the crenellations and down the outer wall of the Spire.

She rapped her fingers on the granite for what must have been the hundredth time that night. And found nothing. The patterns of ice gave no sign that an earthmason had altered the stone.

Disappointed, she was about to give up when she thought of something. Below the dungeon hung the Roots: a dense tangle of moss and dirt and stone that had come along for the journey when the earthmasons, in their haste to escape the floodwaters, had ripped the Spire from its foundation. Could an earthmason have entered the storage room through there? It seemed absurd. The Roots were a deathtrap, ever on the verge of crumbling loose. An earthmason had almost perished trying to repurpose their stone once.

Still, she had to check. Had to be sure.

She signaled for Hendrick to lower her, conscious that he was getting impatient; it had been much longer than two minutes.

The Roots rustled in the wind: a vast, dark mass eager to swallow her with its shifting tendrils. Shona unfastened one of the oil lamps from her harness and raised it to study the clumps of earth that'd refused to fall into the sea for six years.

Her breath caught. Carved into the dirt was a row of thin furrows. Like the marks of claws, or the talons of a siege grappler. Or something else. Gently she ran her fingers through them, surprised by how deep they went. She felt something smooth at the base of a furrow and teased it out with surgical care, thinking any moment a clod of rock would collapse on her.

It was a jade claw, with a jagged end as though broken off.

Allcreator take me.

"There's no way they could've wormed through the Roots." Hendrick was studying the claw at his worktable, his huge shadow on their chamber wall quivering in the lamplight. They spoke in whispers so as not to wake Micah. "No bloody way. The Roots would've collapsed in the attempt."

"A skilled enough earthmason could do it." Shona sipped a cup of hot papaya tea with a blanket wrapped around her. "I suspect *I* could do it, if I were careful enough."

"And seal it after you like that? So there's no trace of you?"

"Sculpting is my specialty, Hendrick. Just as smithing is yours. I am sure it could be done."

"Maybe you're the thief."

His sarcastic tone did not drain the remark of its nastiness, but Shona chose to ignore it.

Hendrick dimmed the lamp. "We should wake the Archmason."

"No. I'm afraid he might suspect us."

"But you said—"

"That he affirmed his trust in me. What else would he say?"

"You're cynical, hummingbird."

"From his standpoint, we're the ones who brought another mouth into the world. If we could be so selfish once, why not again?"

"He'd assume the jade thing was in our possession already. That we'd just pretended to find it. Is that it?"

"We can't prove we did."

Hendrick sighed in resignation. "Keep it to ourselves, then."

Fear lurked at the edge of Shona's awareness while she meditated. Fatigue gnawed at her strength. The Spire seemed to grow heavier by the hour as she focused on the helmstone.

It wasn't until after Reyna had taken Shona's place in the circle—and she was trudging up to her chamber, the cold afternoon light stabbing her eyes—that her fear was free to gain shape.

The thief was not from the Spire.

No matter how many times she turned it over, it sounded mad. But it was the only explanation.

Any earthmasons who could break the moon could survive what comes after.

They're out there, my mountain. We will find them.

"No, you fool of an earthmason. They will find us," she told herself.

But who were *they*? And why—why had they broken the moon? Drowned the world and all creatures in it?

The Spirefolk believed the Allcreator had done it. The earthmasons assumed it was revenge for the lackblooms' tyranny, while the lackblooms held that it was punishment for centuries of decadence, of impiety.

But Shona had never embraced the divine explanation. In her bones, she had always felt that earthmasons somewhere in the world, beyond the reach of love or law, had engineered the cataclysm. It had given her hope. Hope that those earthmasons, however mad or monstrous they might be, were still alive somewhere. That there was still land. Civilization. A chance of rebirth.

A land inhabited by monsters was no paradise, but it was better than death. Anything was better than death.

"An ambush? Are you mad?" Hendrick was smoothing a bent harpoon back into shape at his worktable. "If the thief is what you think, they won't be taken as easy as that."

Shona stood behind him, resting her hands on his shoulders affectionately. "If they were so dangerous, they wouldn't need to use stealth. I have figured it out, Henrick. The thief's an exile. Or a runaway, perhaps. The thing Lorrick and I saw in the sky—it's their *craft*."

"What in the sacred name do you mean?"

"In the days of the Stone Empire, when earthmasons were at the height of power, the scholars imagined we would someday build stone chariots that could fly. Not like the Spire, slow and unwieldy, but something as easy to move as your flesh. Something even the lowest earthmason could maneuver, it would take so little skill."

"That sounds nice. But the Empire fell when we decided it would be more interesting to fight each other. And I doubt any earthmasons since the collapse ever found the trick to bloody sky-ships."

"*Our* Empire fell. But our Empire was not the whole world."

Hendrick set down the harpoon and looked at her. "Wanting to believe that won't make it so."

"Will you help me set up an ambush or not?"

"It's a bad idea. If Tybalt catches you, what will you tell him?"

"The truth," she said, and went to make herself some tea; she would need to keep alert if she hoped to catch the thief.

The stone softened under her hand like clay in the sun, until she could fashion a small hole through it with ease. She peered through the hole: no one in the storage room.

The midwife Imogen, as alert as any earthmason despite her old age, was managing Shona's harness from the lookout. Whenever Hendrick was busy in the meditation circle, Shona relied on Imogen to help her mend the Spire.

Shona had to move quickly lest the midwife suspect she wasn't sealing ice-cracks. After checking that Imogen wasn't looking over the crenellations, Shona expanded the hole she'd made. She grew it until it was big enough to crawl through, then shook a tether for Imogen to unspool her. The ropes of seaweed slackened with a crinkling sound, allowing Shona to worm her way into the storage room.

Inside, she sealed the wall around her tethers, fixing them in place, and got out of her harness quietly. A single oil lamp was flickering, low. She ran her hands across the floor until she found it: a spot one armspan across with no cracks or fissures, as if the stone had been melted down and set anew. Just as she'd anticipated.

She buried the end of a long line of sea silk in the spot— shallowly enough that the thief, while emerging from the Roots, would not notice it before setting it loose— then took the line with her as she got back into her harness and crawled out of the room. She resealed the wall as she went, leaving just enough space for the silk.

Outside, she signaled for Imogen to lift her. When she reached the story she wanted, she climbed partway around the Spire to her chamber window, then clambered through it. She pulled the line of sea silk as taut as she could, tied its other end around a ceramic bowl, and hung the bowl off her bedside table, high enough to shatter when it fell. The next time the thief opened the floor of the storage room, someone in her chamber would hear it.

The next day, Shona arrived at the meditation circle to take Tybalt's place—but Reyna was sitting there instead, her deep eyes ringed with dark circles like those of a nun after a Lunar Fast.

"What do you mean he's *missing?*" Shona whispered to her, once she'd drawn her far enough from the circle that they would not disturb it.

"Tybalt was meant to take my spot in the meditation circle," Reyna explained. "But he never appeared."

Shona tried to squelch the tar-bubble of fear rising in her.

"Did you visit his chamber?"

"Shona, I've looked everywhere. The Archmason's gone."

"Have Gellard take my place for now. I'll return soon."

Shona hurried to the Archmason's chamber on the second story. When her knocks went unanswered, she focused on the reinforced lock—much too dense for one earthmason to break— until the wards inside it clicked home. A trick she'd learned as a vagrant before the Guild of Architects had scraped her up.

Tybalt's cat Despond slipped through her legs as she opened the door. The chamber was even more spartan than Shona's, with a ratty cot, a dust-covered shrine, and not much more. The air smelled of fish stew; the Archmason liked to eat in his room.

She searched the place for signs of a struggle, found none.

She raced back down to the dungeon and into the storage room, surprised it was unlocked. It looked just as she'd left it a day ago. The line of sea silk—as far as she could tell—had not been moved.

There was just one change: a red stain on the floor near the drylocks, no larger than a coin. It might have been nothing— drops of tea that Tybalt had been sipping during his last inspection, perhaps—but Shona suspected it was blood.

"You don't think he…?" Reyna stood in the doorway, voice edged with fear.

"Jumped? Never. Not Tybalt."

Shona had no choice but to tell the Spirefolk.

But the thief—the thief had to stay a secret, until she could prove it was not one of them. They would gorge on the chance to blame each other if she gave it to them.

After hearing the news, the Spirefolk she'd summoned to the feast room—everyone, save the earthmasons in the meditation circle—traded looks of disbelief, of despair. Hendrick kissed Micah's head and whispered something reassuring to her.

Shona's voice chiseled through the silence: "When was the last time any of you saw him?"

Gellard Grey-Eyes lifted his small, sun-cured head. Though not blind, as Shona had assumed once, his eyes had a milky pallor equal to his name, the residue of some affliction in his youth. "I took Tybalt's place in the circle. He went into the storage room to tally up our food, if I remember right. I don't know if he left the room. I was deep in meditation by then."

Cadmus stared at Shona over smooth, steepled hands. "Tybalt and I were not friends, as you know. But I know a hard man from a soft one. The only thing that could have killed him was another earthmason."

Murmurs of agreement filled the room.

"Or a lackbloom with the edge of surprise," said Hendrick. "But we don't know he's dead. We'd be fools to assume it."

"I agree," said Shona.

"Seeing as you're the Archmason until we find him," said Cadmus, "what do you suggest we do?"

"Stay in groups. Avoid the dungeon except to meditate. Keep your eyes open for any trace of Tybalt. And most importantly, do not let his disappearance distract you from your duties. We still have a Spire to maintain."

Old Lorrick ran long fingernails through his beard, his sun-reddened eyes fastened on something only he could see. "All these years searching for land—it's only after that thing in the sky showed up someone disappears. Very curious."

"What are you suggesting?" said Reyna.

"Only that things have taken on a strangeness since we headed north. Can you not feel it?"

"I can feel my head annealing whenever you speak," said Hendrick.

Old Lorrick shot him a look.

"We should resist indulging in superstition," said Shona, trying to channel Tybalt's calm, "when our situation's vexing enough as it is."

Cadmus was watching the clouds change color on the third-story landing outside her chamber. He turned as she came up the stairs, cloak stirring in the chilly air.

"It's a queer thing, but I could swear I heard someone in the harness a few days ago, in the dead of night. Most likely just the wind, of course."

"Most likely, my liege," said Shona, fumbling for the chamber key in her trouser pocket.

"Who would be inspecting the wall at that hour, in such bitter cold?"

She made to open her chamber door when Cadmus touched her shoulder, his dolphinskin glove so soft it might have been air.

"Is there something I can do for you, Cadmus?"

"I don't know what you're hiding. And I don't know why you're hiding it. But I would remind you that secrets don't last long on the Spire. Give Hendrick my regards, Archmason Shona."

He dipped his head in farewell and made his way down the stairs.

Shona untied the ceramic bowl from the line of sea silk and set it on the bedside table.

Hendrick was sitting on the cot, unlacing his boots. The smell of death rose from his feet as soon as they were free.

"It was a clever idea, hummingbird. But you didn't account for the thief being cleverer."

"They must enter the room through a different spot each time. I should have inspected the place more thoroughly."

"Or they sensed the silk as they were coming through. Made sure it didn't come loose."

"Perhaps."

"Seems they really don't want to get caught."

Shona sealed Hendrick's foul-smelling boots in the wall, then collapsed into the cot beside him. She was so tired not even her aches could have kept her from falling asleep if she dared shut her eyes. He ran his great leathery hand over her arms and legs, neck and scalp, checking as always for small blood spots and other signs of the Slow Death. His exhalation held relief, but it was temporary.

"Cadmus confronted me, Hendrick. He knows we're not telling them everything."

"That pompous shit can get tossed to the sharks."

"One lackbloom talks to another. Soon they all want answers."

"So tell them the truth. That an earthmason from outside the Spire's been stealing our food. That Tybalt may've tried to ambush them. May've gotten killed."

Shona looked at him. "You believe me, then."

He nodded. "I didn't want to tell you, but I thought maybe the thief was Tybalt himself till he vanished. He spent more time in the storage room than anyone. I thought maybe—maybe he figured someone would find out, and telling you was his way of protecting himself. I'm ashamed it even crossed my mind."

"I won't pretend it didn't cross mine as well," Shona admitted.

"The thief must be here, right? They've got to set down somewhere. They must be hiding in the walls of the Spire."

"Or *under* it." She sat up, her fatigue swept away by adrenaline. "They're hiding inside the Roots."

"That's madness. It would—"

"Collapse, yes. Unless you're the sort of earthmason who can break moons and fly sky-ships."

Hendrick covered his face, "Allcreator take me. You want to go down there."

"If we're right, do you know what that means?"

He spoke the word tentatively, like a fickle spell. "Land."

"Land," she said. "They'll know the way to land."

"You're mad to even dream of going in that deathtrap."

"I won't deny that, Hendrick."

"And—damn everything—I'm as mad for helping you."

Shona was in charge of the storage room now that she was Archmason, but she felt no less like an intruder entering it without Tybalt's permission. Habits were slow to thaw on the Spire. Inside, Hendrick helped Shona moor the seaweed harness to the wall. It was unlikely anyone would notice it missing at this hour, but Shona still prayed that no one visited the lookout.

When she was finished donning the harness, Hendrick gave her the longknife he'd sharpened that evening, and she strapped it to the harness alongside two oil lamps. A second knife gleamed in Hendrick's belt.

Since the seat of the harness only had room for Shona, Hendrick linked himself to a harness tether for safety, looping one end of an iron chain around it and looping the other end around his belt.

Shona knelt to open a hole in the floor when a fresh fear constricted her.

"What is it?" Hendrick whispered.

She could sense the Roots below them, huge and heavy.

"What if we're wrong? What if there's nothing down here?"

"The thief may've fled already. That's true. But we'll never know unless we look."

And if they captured the thief, what then? How would she handle learning that her kind had drowned the world after all?

The very thought twisted her guts with guilt.

But it was this or death. There was no other way.

Shona carefully formed a hole in the floor, revealing the dark brown surface of the Roots.

She sculpted their path downward in slow, deliberate scoops while Hendrick packed the dirt and rock they displaced back into the walls above them, leaving just enough room for the harness tethers. The deeper they went, the slower they worked, pausing each time a tremor passed through the Roots. The tremors grew louder.

Shona paused to drink from her waterskin, passed it to Hendrick.

"I can sense a pocket over there." One hand on the stone, Shona pointed to a spot perpendicular to their path. "No, there." She adjusted her finger downward. "It's at least as big as our chamber, but I can't tell much more than that."

Hendrick brushed water off his beard. "How far?"

"Too far for the harness. We'll have to leave it behind."

"No." He grabbed her before she could pull the clasps. "Too dangerous. If the ground falls from under you, you're finished. I'll go." He unchained himself from the tethers.

"Hendrick."

"You would leave Micah an orphan?"

"Listen." She took his hand. "Nothing we do here will matter unless we capture this person. And as strong as you are, there is only one of you."

His chewed his lip, looking anguished. But when she took off the harness, he did not stop her.

They tunneled through the earth until the pocket was an armspan ahead of them, seeming to throb under Shona's hands with a hundred possibilities. Her heart was racing; her skin was clammy with sweat.

They both drew their longknives, and Shona opened the last stretch of stone.

It was a room: half again larger than their own, the walls smoothed with great care. A few stone containers rose from the floor, as large as the drylocks in the storage room; the lid of one was askew, letting out the scent of fish. Shona crept into the room with Hendrick, scanning the objects on the floor in wonder: a small midden of fishbones, scuffed clothes made of yellow-grey silk, little white spheres that gave off light, a pair of greaves with jade plating. Atop a shiny black book with strange gold characters across its spine sat a steel-and-glass disc with a twitching needle at its center.

A tunnel led to another room. Inside was Tybalt, lying still.

They rushed to him and pulled him upright. His face was cut, bruised. An elaborate steel brace bound his wrists, and a sharp wire running from its intricate little wards was looped around his throat.

Tybalt's eyes snapped open, bloodshot.

"Shona."

"Thank the Allcreator you're alive. Where are they?"

"Catching fish, I assume. Listen. She is not wicked, I don't think. She—she seems scared."

"We'll decide that for ourselves," said Hendrick. He knelt to cut the brace's wires, but Tybalt flinched away.

"It'll tighten around my throat if you try to break it."

"Is there a key?"

Tybalt shook his head. "All magic. Their metalcraft is unlike anything I've seen. She has a—a flying thing. Allcreator take me; if I'd known what we were dealing with, I would not have ambushed her."

"What does she want?" asked Shona.

"We have tried to communicate, but it is difficult. Her language is unfamiliar to me, though not entirely. Some words I know; I am not sure why. She has escaped from something or someone, I think. She has the air of one who has endured many ordeals."

"Do you know where she came from?"

"No. But she does not look—well, like us."

Before Shona could ask what he meant, the Roots shuddered slightly as if something had struck them. She fashioned an alcove in the wall and pulled Hendrick into it, then sealed it closed save for a hole to peer through.

The sound of stone parting. Then, footsteps.

A small, hunched woman shuffled into the room, pulling off a suit of jade armor one piece at a time. Her skin was pale as a moon-shard and crisscrossed with paler scars, and her hair flowed down fine and white as asbestos when she removed her jade helm. She might have been a hundred years old until she turned her head, and then looked no older than a maiden, with a perfectly smooth face but for a pair of slanted scars. Her eyes were huge. One had a black pupil so large it seemed a hole in her head; the other was a ball of neatly etched jade.

As the woman approached Tybalt, clutching a fat brown fish like a cudgel, Shona was certain the woman would hear her heartbeat through the wall.

"Fel," said Tybalt. "If you let me go, I could be more useful to you."

Fel mumbled something in a harsh tongue and tossed the fish to Tybalt. Then she hauled a cask of water into the room. Her back turned to Shona, she poured the water into a stone basin she'd made, then ripped the salt from it in a sweeping motion and drank with animal fervor, head bowed and slurping.

Shona opened the wall quietly, and she and Hendrick moved toward the stranger in slow, tentative steps, spreading out to flank her. Were Shona more skillful, she could have drawn the stone from the drinking basin around Fel's legs to trap her. But her magic was too weak at that distance.

She had to settle for barbarism. Focusing, she levitated the longknife with her magic and guided it silently toward a spot behind Fel's spine, holding it in place there; Hendrick levitated his own blade behind Fel's heart, so that it looked as though a pair of invisible assassins were on the cusp of ending her.

"We do not wish you harm," said Shona, praying Fel understood her tone if not her words. "Please do not move."

Fel went stone-still. Then, in defiance of Shona and Hendrick, the knives edged back from Fel slightly as she turned around, baring neat jade teeth. Tiny colorful piercings sparkled in her nose, cheeks, eyebrows.

"Stay calm," said Hendrick, holding up his palms in restraint.

To Shona's horror, the knives began to glide toward her and Hendrick, glimmering, steady as hate.

"Calm." Fel rolled the word in her mouth like a bitter morsel of something.

Shona and Hendrick pushed back as hard as they could, but it did not matter; the knives drew closer, and closer still. Hendrick swiped to grab one, but the hilt twisted out of reach. Fel laughed: a cruel sound, thick with contempt.

Allcreator save us if this fails.

Shona dropped to her hands, flinging her strength into the ground. The stone cracked with a thunderclap; tremors surged through the Roots. Fel let the knives drop with a startled gasp and reached down to keep the floor from collapsing. Hendrick lunged at her, slamming her against the wall. She sucked in air through squeezed pipes and sprang a stubby jade spike from a knuckle, then stabbed Hendrick's abdomen, twisting into it. Blood bloomed through his work-smock, dark as wine.

Shona grabbed the spike-arm and pinned it to the wall. Fel tried to scream, but Hendrick had her locked in a sleeping grip. In seconds, she slumped to the ground, unconscious.

The Roots rumbled and shook. A slab of floor fell away to reveal a patch of night-black ocean. Cold air sucked Shona's hair toward the hole as she tried to close it. Tybalt helped her, reaching with bound hands until the ground resealed. Slowly, the tremors subsided.

Hendrick sat against the wall, clutching his wound. Shona's throat tightened at the sight of it.

"I'll be fine," he said. "The healer can fix it."

Tybalt shook his head. "There is no chance of climbing up in that condition."

"Don't be so optimistic."

But Tybalt was right. Shona would have to make the journey alone.

"If that—that *thing* moves so much as a finger, don't hesitate to knock her out again," she said.

With Tybalt's help, she found the sky-craft in a carefully sculpted tunnel sealed off from the other rooms. She remembered the running paths that some birds used to gain momentum for flight, and assumed the tunnel held a similar purpose.

The craft was made of jade and wood and canvas, with a pair of long, hinged wings folded up against its flanks and a carriage just large enough for one. It stood on two legs with sharp-clawed feet. One claw was broken off.

Shona climbed into the craft and concentrated on its wings. The jade fixtures bent to her will with surprising readiness, dragging the wood and canvas parts with them as they shifted into a slow flapping motion. But as soon as she tried to move the legs, her hold on the wings slipped, and they fell limp. Controlling both at once did not seem possible.

She felt around inside the carriage— and found a device chained to the wall. It was a crystal sphere about the size of her fist, and it held a jade model of the craft on a metal spindle. She was baffled until she thought of the helmstone that held up the Spire. A depression at the front of the craft clicked as Shona placed the sphere inside it. She focused on the little model, on moving its wings and legs at once. The craft mirrored the movements.

So that was the trick.

She walked the craft across the tunnel to get a feel for it, then back again. It felt slow and heavy, and after some missteps she thought it might be safer to climb back up the Roots. But a fresh surge of tremors quashed that idea.

She opened a path to the sky, then took a running jump into the void, willing the craft's wings to flap hard against the icy skirling air. A swelling gust tried to flip her instantly, like a shove from a drunken brawler, and the mirrored starlight on the water disoriented her, wrecking what was left of her balance. She felt herself swerving into endless night, dizzy, panic stabbing her thin bubble of concentration. She was falling, falling into a chasm of stars.

Fly. Fly. Fly.

But the wind chanted, "Fall, fall, fall," as it swatted her and hammered her and whipped her.

She kept her mind on the model in the crystal sphere. Now that she was too far from the Spire's light to see it clearly, she could focus on the weight of the craft and on the movement of the wings, as if she were sitting shut-eyed in a meditation circle. And the craft steadied itself, wobbling. She forced the wings to flap harder, harder. Veering a little, she saw the dwindling silhouette of the Spire, ink-black but for faint specks of lamplight, and flew toward it.

She alighted on the lookout harder than intended, causing the craft to creak and shudder. Relief flooded her chest as she jumped to the ground—followed by a sudden wave of fear.

Cadmus was standing before the stairway entrance in his everyday clothes, clutching his cloak tight around himself for warmth. An oil lamp rested on the ground beside him, as though he'd been waiting for her.

His mouth moved a few times before words came out.

"I don't—I cannot quite believe it," he said, approaching the craft, the golden pommel of his ancestral sword glinting like sunlight from under his cloak.

As soon as she took a step toward the entrance, his hand went to the sword, as if afraid she would grab it with her magic. It was a reasonable fear.

"Hendrick's hurt," she said, almost pleading. "I need to get help."

"Something's found us, haven't they?"

She hesitated. "Yes."

"I knew it. I knew you were hiding something. And when I saw that the harness was missing, I knew you were scheming with that brute. But *this*," he said, marveling at the craft, "I could not have guessed at this. What numinous beings have found us, Shona? A seraph of the Allcreator? As liege lord of the cleanfolk, I deserve to know."

She thought of Hendrick bleeding out in the Roots, and of the sword under Cadmus's cloak. Thought of how its castle-forged edge might feel against her flesh if she were too slow or too clumsy to stop it. She had seen that sword used only once, during the Incident. Had seen the clean red path it had made through the earthmason—a miner no older than herself—who had tried to stab him with a longknife. The sound had been wet and final; she did not wish to hear it again.

"A survivor of the deluge, like ourselves," she said. "Not a god. Not a seraph. Just an earthmason, like me and Hendrick and Tybalt."

"You would insult my wits by claiming a *mudrat* made this vessel?"

"She's down in the Roots right now, unconscious for the moment. I can take you down to see her—my liege."

The anger on his face melted away as he studied the craft more carefully, taking in its intricate construction. And the expression that replaced it was something else altogether. Fear. He was afraid that she was telling the truth.

He swallowed, looking slightly sick, and shook his head in disbelief. But he said nothing more after that, and made no move to stop her as she hurried to the stairway.

A minute later, the healer, a fat man wrapped in a thick sharkskin blanket, was rubbing his half-open eyes as he answered the door.

"Alucart," she said, "I need your help."

She roused Gellard Grey-Eyes next, explaining in a breathless rush everything she could compress into the seconds afforded to her, and the three of them raced down to the dungeon, past the meditation circle, into the storage room, where the seaweed harness, its tethers still snaking down into the hole from their moorings, awaited them.

"Is there really no other way?" Alucart asked as Shona pulled up the harness.

"It does seem quite dangerous," Gellard concurred.

Biting down contempt, Shona rounded on them. "Do you imagine for a moment that Hendrick or Tybalt would not do the same for you? Well, do you?"

The men traded looks of equal parts shame and dread.

Then Alucart quickly took the harness and donned it.

"I'm just a lackbloom," he said defensively. "I can't bend fucking rocks if the Roots start collapsing, can I?"

Gellard was slower at digging than Hendrick had been, but Shona had practice now and remembered the path to Fel's chamber.

When they emerged, the men gasped in wonder.

"What in the sacred name is this place?" asked Gellard.

"I did tell you," said Shona.

"And I—I thought I believed you. Truly, I did."

Tybalt looked up at the sound of their voices, his face awash with relief. "You'd better hurry, Hendrick's losing a lot of blood."

Shona's heart sank at how pale Hendrick had become. Sweat glazed his brow. His hands were failing to stanch the wound even slightly.

Without hesitation, Alucart opened his instrument case and went to work. Hendrick winced as the healer poured a precious half-cup of wine on his wound. "Hold still, you restless orangutan. You want me to sew this shut properly or not?"

Shona wasted no time in binding Fel from head to foot in seaweed rope, taking care to cover her eyes. She tied her hands tightest, afraid that Fel would cut through her bonds with other things hidden inside her. Only death could stop a skilled earthmason from moving stone, but restricting sight and movement made their magic less precise. It wasn't perfect, but it would serve until Shona could seal Fel in a proper room and place some earthmasons around her.

Gellard hoisted Fel over his shoulder like a sack of gravel, trudged back toward the hole they'd come down.

Shona kissed Hendrick's warm, damp forehead as he was being mended, knowing it would be an arduous climb back up the Roots without his help.

"Be strong, my mountain," she said. "Once Fel is safely contained, we will come back for you and Tybalt."

"That's good to hear," he mumbled through a haze of delirium, and laughed.

A few days later, the Spire was a different place. The walls were thrumming with frenzied conversation, and Fel—strange, mysterious Fel—was still bound up like a bedlamite on the third story with several earthmasons guarding her.

And Shona, too tired to even feel it anymore, was sitting beside Hendrick in bed, while he spooned fish stew into his mouth in hungry slurps. His recovery had been quicker than she'd expected, and her heart sang a little whenever he awoke from one of his deep, precarious sleeps. Alucart came by three times each day to change Hendrick's dressings.

"I owe you my life," Hendrick had told him one morning.

"We can discuss repayment when we find land," Alucart had replied.

The Spirefolk knew what was at stake now. Shona had told them everything she could afford to tell. Every face in the feast room had drifted through a dozen shades of astonishment as she gave her account of recent events, from the missing food to Tybalt's kidnapping and her struggle to find him. She left out her belief—and now Hendrick's—that Fel's civilization had broken the moon. But now the Spirefolk knew that others had survived the deluge, that there must be land, and most of them rejoiced in this knowledge.

Most, but not all. Some wondered why Fel had left her refuge in the first place.

And why her kin would welcome eighty-two new bellies to fill.

Hendrick wasn't one of the worriers. He sighed in contentment as Shona scratched a spot on his back beyond his reach, then plopped back in the cot. He was looking a hundred times livelier since Alucart had tended to him.

"I love you more than the Allcreator, did you know that?"

"You're talking a lot more today. That's good," said Shona, setting his half-finished bowl of fish stew on the bedside table.

He winced while adjusting himself, then closed his eyes with a tired smile.

Tybalt came to visit, looking haggard as death but grateful to be free of the brace. It had been a simple offer to Fel: "Remove the brace if you want to eat." And after three days without food, she had taken it. Shona had feared what Fel would do once the rope was untied momentarily from her eyes and hands. But any urge to rebel must have withered at the sight of half the earthmasons in the Spire surrounding her. So, carefully adjusting the wards, Fel had removed the device from Tybalt's neck and wrists, taking perhaps longer than needed. Now Tybalt could not stop rubbing the red line imprinted on his throat, like a man who'd escaped a hanging at the last moment.

Hendrick sat up as Tybalt stepped into the bedroom. "Archmason."

"Not anymore," said Tybalt. "I have ceded that burden to Shona. I am old and weary, and it is my right."

Hendrick looked at Shona. "You didn't tell me that."

Shona shrugged. "I did. But I don't think you heard it."

"How are you feeling?" Tybalt asked Hendrick.

"To tell you the truth, bored."

"Well, enjoy it while you can."

Tybalt pulled a book out of his sharkskin satchel: the black one with gold characters that Shona had glimpsed among the stranger's artifacts.

"Fel still refuses to learn our tongue," he said. "It will take some time to communicate. But I have studied this item carefully, and I think you should know what I have found, Archmason."

Gently, as though handling a delicate instrument, he opened the book. Hundreds of silvery pages swished apart to reveal surfaces slate-blank but for snatches of light or shadow where creases had formed.

"Beautiful, isn't it?"

"Are those pages made of—metal?" said Hendrick.

Tybalt nodded. "Yet softer than any parchment, and that's not the strangest thing about them. Shona, would you care to close the window shutters? And cover the gaps with a blanket, if you would."

Once the room was dark, Tybalt procured something from his pocket which began to glow, illuminating his face at ghoulish angles. It was one of the light-spheres that belonged to Fel.

"Look," he whispered.

Shona and Hendrick leaned over the book. To Shona's astonishment, thousands of jagged white characters—not unlike those of the Diamantine Script of the Stone Empire—had appeared on the pages.

"Impressed? Well, that's not half of it. Observe." Tybalt moved the light-sphere in a slow clockwise fashion over the pages. And as he did, the characters transformed —once, twice, three times—before settling back into their original shapes where the rotation ended. "Four overlapping texts, do you see? A most economical way to make a book."

"Ingenious," said Hendrick, his face bright with interest.

Shona nodded in agreement.

"My grasp of the Diamantine Script is much too weak to tease out more than a few traces of meaning, alas," said Tybalt.

"So it *is* the ancient script," murmured Shona, not quite believing it.

"A distant offspring of it, anyway. Yes, I know what you're thinking. I see it in your eyes. And it appears to be true. *The Stone Empire did not fall.* Not completely. But you need not take my word."

He flipped to another place in the book, and an illustration more dazzling than any Shona had ever seen—either in the temple manuscripts that had once filled the capital, or in the murals that had emblazoned the lackblooms' high manse walls—flooded the darkness with shimmering colors, each touched with a silvery tint like a rainbow poured through mercury.

The illustration showed a thin, steepled mountain rising from an icy waste. And as Tybalt moved the light-sphere, slowly, very slowly, a throng of people—hundreds of them, men and women and children—

seemed to trudge toward the mountain from outside the page. Bundled in filthy rags, they dragged with them dogs and horses and onagers, huge wagons piled with goods. Shona recognized their diamond sigils.

"Remnants of the Stone Empire," she said.

"So it seems," said Tybalt. "This mountain—I cannot be sure just yet, not until I have studied the script more carefully—but I do believe this mountain is where we will find Fel's people, if there are more of them."

"The ones who broke the moon," Hendrick muttered to Shona, and she nodded in wonder. They had to be.

Days passed, then weeks, as the Spire drifted further north, into emptinesses colder and cloudier, where the daylight seemed to drag its feet. And every morning and evening, when she was not meditating, Shona went to the lookout to scan the horizon.

When Hendrick was fully recovered, he joined her too, sometimes hoisting Micah on his back to see above the crenellations, her red hair whipping like fire in the icy wind. No one complained of the cold or the wind. All that mattered was the horizon.

But it was fine and crisp as a sword's edge—no mountain in sight.

After a month of searching, Shona's hopes began to fade. Fel, in her maddening silence, was no more useful than a statue, and Tybalt's progress in deciphering the book had proven painfully slow.

But Shona was always the last one on the lookout, even as the dwindling light of dusk made the distance inscrutable.

This night was no different. Hendrick had left her with a kiss, and had taken his warmth with him down to bed, and now she was alone atop the Spire with the shadows hardening around her, and with the stars and the moon-shards stretching like strange, luminous silt-plumes in that second ocean above her.

A cold gale whistled sadly through the crenellations, flicking back her sleeves and scorching her raw face for a moment, and she wrapped her arms around herself, as if this would help. She felt like the walls of the Spire just then, weak and tired and cracked from the cold. She belonged in bed with Hendrick, she thought, and turned to leave.

But as she did, she caught a flicker out of the corner of her eye—and paused, feeling the same small tug on her awareness as when she'd glimpsed Fel's craft for the first time, though she had not known it then.

She leaned out over the crenellations, searching the horizon.

The flicker came again, stronger—a thin orange light, not like the silver-white of the stars. A wisp of cloud was half-obscuring it. And then it wasn't, and the light grew with her certainty, its faint aura limning a thin, steepled shape that rose from the distant water.

Her heart was thudding so loud she could not hear the wind anymore. Could not feel the stone beneath her, either; she seemed to be hovering above it, as if in a dream.

But it wasn't a dream. It was real.

They had found land.

*See Jordan Chase-Young's story "Shards"
online at Metaphorosis.
If you liked it, leave a comment. Authors love
that!
Remember to subscribe to our e-mail updates so
you'll know when new stories are posted.*

About the story

I've always suspected that magic, if it existed, would be a profound threat to human survival. It would empower tyrants, create lasting fault lines between groups, and permit destruction on a vast scale. But magic would also afford great opportunities. It would cut down on drudgery, make life more interesting, and in the right hands allow for great progress. "Which of the two would win out?" I've wondered. "Would magic help humanity grow, or would it doom us?"

This story flowed out of that question. I thought of a world in which some people could manipulate stone with magic, could shape it to their will. It seemed only a matter of time before some of them, somewhere, used that magic to destroy the world. But not the whole world, not everyone. Some people would use that magic to survive, to keep humanity aloft in the teeth of despair. And maybe—who knows?—that second group would win out in the end. Such things are not written in stone.

I don't even remember how many times I rewrote the story from scratch to give you the version you see here. I could put together a fat volume with just the half-drafts, false starts, and jettisoned endings. By the time I submitted the story to Metaphorosis, in December 2018, it had already gone through many rewrites; by the time it was sold, it had gone through several more, each one stronger than the last. As a result of all this editing, I've learned more about the craft of fiction writing than from every book I've read on the subject put together.

I've also learned a lot about my strengths and weaknesses as a writer, and about the deep weirdness of creativity; several times I thought a problem in the story was intractable, only to realize, with a jolt of surprise, that the answer was sitting in front of me all along. In earlier drafts, for example, the main character's motives, role in the Spire, and family members, together with the nature of the Spire, the magic system, and the world, were doled out in a slow, serial sequence, which hurt the pacing greatly; I realized I could fix that problem with ease by smashing all those elements together in the first couple of scenes. One of the joys of writing is having revelations like these.

A question for the author

Q: When do you decide a story is finished?

A: The splendid curse—the maddening blessing—of fiction is that a story is never finished. As David

Deutsch taught us, any artwork is infinitely perfectible; you could spend millions of years improving a story one word, sentence, or scene at a time, but the combinatorially unbounded nature of thought means you'd still be infinitely far from perfection!

So if you can't finish a story, really finish it, the question is when to abandon it. I have a poetic answer and a practical one. The poetic answer: I decide a story is finished when it makes me feel unadulterated pride to read it from beginning to end. The prose is clear and smooth, the action is balanced and organic, the characters have full voices and satisfying arcs, and the ending leaves one with a frisson of wonder and the feeling of time well spent. The practical answer: I decide a story is finished when I can no longer see how to improve it. Oh, I know there are improvements to be made, glorious ones just around the edge of thought, but I don't yet have the knowledge to find them. So I finish the story and start working on another, in the hopes of getting better.

About the author

Jordan Allan Chase-Young was machine-pressed into a science-fiction and fantasy writer by the cold grey skies of Oregon, where he spent most of his life. Now he is gingerly avoiding buff kangaroos and kamikaze magpies in the strange desolation of Australia, with his wife and one cactus, while reading and writing speculative fiction more ardently than ever—that is, when not nose-deep in texts about history, economics, future studies, or global catastrophic risk in search of why civilizations thrive or flounder. He is mostly optimistic about humanity's potential to turn the dead, quiet universe outside our pale blue dot into a living, thinking one. He enjoys hiking, video games, Twitter, astrobiology, and illustration, and wishes he had more time to draw like he used to.

cbookofthenewsun.wordpress.com, @jachaseyoung

A Picture of Home, in Silence

Alexandra Seidel

The soles on Sam's first pair of shoes are worn and cracked, and she is tired. She craves rest, because the way home is long. Light reflects off tall stained glass windows, and because there were none of those in the research colony, Sam is curious, stops, walks away from the road, and enters the building.

Years and miles ago, when Sam first came to the research colony, she was useful, and being useful helped keep her mind from drifting to the past. Sam knew how to use a microscope, how to navigate a lab, how to read colored graphs and the hues of chemical indicators. She thought she'd never leave the research colony, would live there and find happiness with the other survivors, with all the others who had been uprooted by the silence of loss like herself.

A month before Sam decided to leave, she was told to stay out of the lab, to take care of herself instead, to let others pursue as work what Sam pursues as love. They did not call her redundant, not to her face. To her face, they offered silent compassion. It took Sam a month to realize the research colony was not home, never had been, to realize she was never going back to the lab and would never find the kind of happiness to replace the science, the kind of happiness that warms the skin like touch. To understand in her heart as well as her head that the loss of sight was final. When she left the research colony at the end of that month and had to walk through the fields of silence, the fields where those that never were invited inside still lay as plunder for the ravens, Sam knew she would never return, because some of the silence would always cast an echo into the colony itself.

Much of the glass in the church is broken, but some of the windows still hold their ancient pictures. Sam wipes the dust of disuse from a spot in the pews and sits, looks from her scuffed shoes that were new not too long ago up to the pictures. She doesn't know what the painted glass is meant to tell her, but the wonder of people, even glass people, is striking. The glass world, the world the windows show, seems full and colorful, as if it stretches, as if you could meet another person around every corner. The light is dyed in colors and spills the images over the dirty church floor, a kaleidoscope copy of the windows themselves. This bright shadow of colored light makes Sam forget that glass worlds, all worlds, are brittle.

The windows make touch look normal, ordinary. The last time Sam was touched by another human was almost three months ago. They took her blood, and they wore gloves. There are antibodies in her blood, just like there should be in those that survived an infection. If Sam concentrates, she can feel her arm grow warm from the touch. Even after all this time, the memory of touch still lingers while the memory of sight has dulled, the faces overexposed by time. Nothing in Sam's blood is responsible for Sam's fading vision, that's genetic. She barely felt the needle rip her skin when they took her blood. It was the touch she felt.

Sam is one of the lucky ones. She was young, barely in school three years, when the diseases spread, two viruses that crossed paths in the bleeding bowels of humanity like two edges of the same sword. Her mother and father were both scientists, her father was a doctor. They understood the need to stay away from where people gathered, malls, playgrounds, fairs, the outside world. Everything Sam knows she owes to her parents, who taught her to read and write, to love math and science.

Many of Sam's generation only learned reading and writing and science once they settled in the research colony, and most of them never learned to love those things. Back home, before the colony, Sam had seen her parents love them, and so that love came easy to her as well.

A flyer rests under a layer of dust, an arm's length from where Sam is sitting and staring at the glass. *The end is nigh*, it warns. The end is already past and done. Sam, like most survivors her age, came to the research colony an orphan.

Sam looks at the windows and the silent shards below them where stories lie scattered; test tubes scattered on the floor, broken, because she didn't see, that's how it started. "Glass, like touch, can cut," Sam says, startled by the echo the building offers. The doctor, when he told Sam of the unavoidable loss of sight, held her hand where the broken test tubes had sliced it open, and of that touch, Sam remembers only pain. Her need for rest smothered by the memory of loss, she picks up the flyer, tears it in two, and leaves the empty room to the play of shadow and light.

It has gotten easier, the walking. Sam is on her second pair of shoes. It is an open garden gate and not the need for rest that pulls her away from the road, because the wrought curls of metal flowers shake a memory loose in Sam's mind: the garden gate at home where she grew up and learned to love science looks exactly like this. Sam's father once decorated it with balloons for her birthday, yellow and red and blue ones. Past the gate, the air smells sweet, and a house sits there, shaded by trees.

Sam would have tried the front door, but humming makes her take a garden path overgrown with weeds. When she sees the beekeeper, Sam stops, stunned at the presence of another survivor. The beekeeper turns, sees Sam, but doesn't stop in her work. Sam approaches.

"I do not get visitors," the beekeeper says.

Sam nods, uncertain whether the beekeeper's voice is reproachful or annoyed.

"I'm from the research colony. I was walking by, then I saw the open garden gate."

The beekeeper examines her, the woman's strange hat dipping down and going up. "So you walked all the way here? I considered going myself when they broadcast their invitation, but I liked it here. You must have been walking for months." Constant humming sheathes the beekeeper even more than her bee suit, the hat with the dark veil, the pale overalls. The garden is lush, glossy, a contrast to the almost uncanny guardian of bees.

"I wanted to do it. And I'm used to the walking by now."

The beekeeper is old. Not *old*, exactly. Gray age didn't survive the viruses. *Relatively speaking, she is old*, Sam's father would have said. Sam can hardly make out the lines of the beekeeper's face behind the veil, but what she sees is harsh and hard, and the humming doesn't hide it.

"You could have taken a car. Surely they have those still running up there in the research colony."

There is disapproval in the beekeeper's voice, distaste, when she says *research colony*. On an intellectual level, Sam understands that not every survivor wishes to come to the colony, that some brave the world alone or in small groups. Sam used to think it an unfathomable choice, the loneliness, the memories lurking around every corner, but seeing the beekeeper now, a part of Sam reconsiders.

After all, I left.

The beekeeper opens a hive and pulls out a wax-encrusted slab. Honey trails the frame and falls to the ground. The bees buzz. To Sam, who doesn't dare come closer, they sound angry, for they have been disturbed.

A bee flies over to Sam's hand. The bee lands on the knuckle of Sam's index finger, and Sam holds her breath the way one does before a kiss. She lets the insect explore, taste her summer warm skin. The bee's colors amaze Sam, so much detail in such a small body, and Sam tries to taste the details with her failing sight as if the yellow and black bands were rare candy. "I don't know how to drive."

This makes the beekeeper chuckle, a noise like the humming of her bees. "It's really not that hard when there's no traffic. Come, let's eat." She carries the honeycombed frame into her house. Inside, the house feels hollow. It makes Sam wonder what a single bee would do with one of the beekeeper's frames all to herself.

Past the threshold, the house is full of echoes. "Did you always live here?" Sam asks.

The beekeeper takes off her hat. A bee falls to the ground, dead. "No. But it's a good place. Lots of stairs, though. Did you ever think of just stopping?"

Sam shakes her head. "No. I want to go back home. Not the colony, home before that. And walking isn't all that bad; you see so much." So many colors, so many shapes. Sam would never abandon the sights to either side of the road. She wants to see as much of a world she never traveled as she can before her sight is lost.

The beekeeper's veil also veils her view of the reality outside of her hives and her honey, Sam realizes as the black gauze of it brushes against the floor and settles next to the dead bee.

"I guess that's true," says the beekeeper as she slips her pale bee suit off. It is a hiding place, this suit, Sam realizes. More dead bees hit the floor, joining the one next to the hat.

Sam cannot help staring. The way the beekeeper moves reminds Sam of the small insects themselves, of the vibrato of their wings, the strange geometry of their dance. The beekeeper catches her watching and smiles, an expression that seems foreign to her face. The house is full of echoes, even if no bees live inside.

The slickness of the beekeeper's honey still clings to Sam's skin, but she had to leave, knew from the moment she heard the echoes that she could not stay in that house and pretend it was a hive. The morning after, the beekeeper left the bed and put on her suit, and Sam felt the touches they had exchanged fade to memory and glass.

The beekeeper had hardly any books in her house, and those that slept on the shelves hadn't been hers. Sam did not feel bad about taking some of them after she put on shoes to continue her walk.

Rain pours down on Sam. It has done so for about an hour, and the beekeeper's house, the beekeeper's bed, would be welcome now that Sam is properly frozen through, even if the beekeeper never shed her suit again. Even the research colony would be welcome.

Sam shakes her head, dislodges raindrops from her hood, memories from her head, and false desires from her heart. No, the beekeeper's bed would not be welcome, that bed was a lonely frame made to hold only a single bee, and the colony would not be welcome either; without the lab, the research colony is just an empty bed in a small apartment ruled by silence. Not even two thousand people live in the colony.

Sam stops in the downpour. There is no sound but the rain, and the rain does little to mute that looming silence in this largely humanless world. Sam screams at the top of her lungs. Her scream doesn't scare animals, because they were smart enough to find shelter from the rain, but it feels good, being noisy. Even if no one else knows about it. Even if the scream, like a koan, might be a noise without a sound.

Bruises are a marvel of color. They are a marvel of pain, too, but the colors fascinate Sam. They start with the reds of freshly torn vessels, then fade to purplish hues of blues and blacks before the skin emerges under greenish yellows. Sam's vision is getting worse, and so the number of bruises she gets to examine increases. She is on her fourth pair of shoes.

Today she stops at a park for food she took off a shelf half a pair of shoes ago. Tearing the plastic gives Sam a moment, just that moment between the plastic being whole and then not, when she can imagine the world never changed. In that moment, there exists the possibility that life so far has been a bad dream, that once the plastic is torn, there will be another plastic-portioned morsel to be grabbed just around the corner.

The food inside tastes like the sacred past of a birthday party and colorful balloons, like an invitation on the garden gate. The taste stirs these memories like glass, stained, broken, and containing a world within: friends from school in pigtails and with chocolate lining their lips. Party hats. Enough candy to fill the largest bowl in the kitchen.

As she eats, Sam distracts herself from crying by tracing the shadows the sunlight casts as it breaks through wild growing trees and grasses that have even conquered half of the bench Sam sits on. She chews slowly and doesn't think about her friend who laughed and wore a party hat and years later kissed Sam until she blushed, because now, that friend is silent and dead.

"I am eating a museum piece," Sam tells a red chested bird that has decided to land on the bench next to her, curious. "Would you also like to eat parts of this exhibit?" She breaks off crumbs and places her offering in front of the bird, who tries it, then looks up at her for more. The bird's eyes and clawed feet are blurry, the colors that dye its feathers unset watercolors. "You can't be greedy, you have to savor this," Sam says, but shares with the bird all the same.

After the food, Sam pulls a book from her backpack, the last one she still carries with her from the beekeeper's house. Her nose almost touches the page, and she squints to make the words come into focus. Sam reads aloud to the bird the story of a girl not unlike Sam, a girl walking a road that promises magic at its end. The bird flies off somewhere in the middle of the last chapter, but Sam reads all of it out loud regardless as if her tongue were trying to cast the letters' shapes into her memory.

When Sam is done reading, and the girl in the story has reached the end of the road, which is not magic at all, just home, Sam knows she should leave the book there instead of carrying unnecessary weight. She thinks she has learned this, not to carry her losses with her and burden herself with stories that are but silence after the last page is read, but she cannot bear to leave the book.

Sunset would always bring the brightest colors, and Sam loves it best of all the times of day. She can make out the colors still, even if the lines the clouds draw in the fading light have gone blurry. Sam no longer reads, and while she manages not to cry for sunsets, today she is finally crying for books.

It is the first time she has cried since she was told her vision would go; the tears seem to have waited, to have gathered, and now they cannot be stopped.

She sits down on a couch that isn't hers in a house that isn't hers, with a book she found there open on her lap. Her eyes just will not let her read it. The pages give her only silence, no more words, and no more stories. And so Sam cries and cries. She falls asleep on the couch, and in the morning she puts the silent book she'll never read aside, focuses on walking instead.

There are smells of grass and pollen, earth. She tries to feel the ground beneath her feet, soft grass, asphalt, gravel. She has found a stick by the road, and finally resigns herself to using it to navigate the world. When she could still read, Sam did not submit to relying on a stick, but now that her books are gone, she allows herself this crutch.

It will not be long now, not long at all, until darkness falls.

The garden wall is too high to climb, but the gate is still unlocked. For a moment, the touch of the gate's iron makes Sam remember the beekeeper, who might have forgotten Sam the morning she left; after all, they only shared one night.

The gate opens easily at first, then sticks a little, just like Sam remembers. She had not thought that she would ever return here, to the place where she grew up. When she left this place, she had thought that she would find a new home in the research colony, a home and something meaningful to do, a home filled with shared happiness. When her feet start down the garden path, Sam remembers that she knew happiness here: party hats, balloons, the sour-sweet novelty of her first crush. Learning to love science. She also remembers silence.

That day, the silence had woken her. The painful sounds of hard-won breathing had gone, and outside, the demands of ravens echoed. That day, Sam had found herself an orphan. The proof lay there on soft pillows, blanket-wrapped, and in her memory, Sam's own cries turned to haunting echoes. She fled from the memory as if it were a weight she shouldn't carry, but silence cannot be outrun. Like the girl in the story Sam read to the bird, Sam's own road ends where it started.

The gate creaks, a sharp, bright noise of metal. The garden path echoes back Sam's footfalls and the regular tapping of her stick. She will find something better than this stick; the attic is full of things, things her father stashed there from his practice. The attic will smell of dust and warmth now, and Sam is already looking forward to being up there. She is looking forward already to taking off her shoes.

As Sam reaches the steps that lead up to the front door, the scent of lilies welcomes her. Her mother planted these, years ago, and on an impulse, Sam turns toward where she knows the flowers grow. Her hands find them even closer than she expects, the heads bobbing toward her in the wind. Sam kneels in the dirt and reaches for them. She doesn't remember what color they are. The petals are soft, and Sam brushes her lips across them, sure that pollen will line her hands. She kisses the flower, a kiss meant for the woman that planted them.

The vibrato of wings brushes against her lips, and Sam remembers a body banded yellow and black. The insect hums, but does not move to reward Sam's kiss with a sting.

Sam pulls back, but the hum follows her as she climbs the steps and opens the door, goes inside. There will be no insect bodies scattered in her home, Sam swears, no echoes loud inside the house, and no more shattering silence. She feels around, familiarizing her arms and feet with corners and furniture. Sam remembers easily where things are, and with the bee humming, she realizes that she has already forgotten her tiny, silent apartment back at the colony.

Sam takes off her backpack, places it by the stairs and pulls out the book, the last she ever read. She finds her way to the family room to place the book on the mantel, right next to the picture frames. When she feels light fall inside through the window glass, Sam smiles and begins to hum along with the bee, the melody of home.

*See Alexandra Seidel's story "A Picture of
Home, in Silence" online at Metaphorosis.
If you liked it, leave a comment. Authors love
that!
Remember to subscribe to our e-mail updates so
you'll know when new stories are posted.*

About the story

I wrote "A Picture of Home, in Silence" in early 2020. At the time, COVID-19 hadn't yet started dominating our everyday lives. Like many of my stories, this one started with a specific image, the main character looking at the stained glass windows and about how light breaks those colors into picture, and it grew from there.

A question for the author

Q: Do you ever feel bad for what you put your characters through?

A: Not really. Under my pseudonym, Alexa Piper, I created a character once that seemed like a boring, two-dimensional villain, so I gave them a backstory and someone who loved them. That character became harder to dispatch, but dispatch them I did.

About the author

Alexandra Seidel spent many a night stargazing when she was a child. These days, she writes stories and poems and drinks a lot of coffee (too much, some say). As Alexa Piper, she writes erotic romance that also leans toward the fantastical. You can follow her on Twitter @Alexa_Seidel or like her Facebook page (https://www.facebook.com/AlexaSeidelWrites/), and find out what she's up to at alexandraseidel.com.

The Chorley

Rachel Ayers

Little Annamarie wore a mournful expression. "Mama," she said, "I can't find my Chorley." Chorley was a ragged stuffed elephant that the girl had had since she was two.

"Where did you leave it?" the Mama asked, the air of distraction hardened on her features. She had taken off the VR glasses that she customarily wore throughout the long hours of the day, and even the child could see that she was irritated by the interruption.

"If I knowed, I wouldn't be sad," the girl pointed out.

"Knew," Mama corrected.

Annamarie stamped her foot. "Mama, I need my Chorley."

Mama sighed and turned away from her desk. "Child, I'm very busy with a big project. If you need your toy right now, you'll have to look for it."

She went back to tinkering with the things on her worktable: an odd assortment of wires and pentacles and computer chips and silver. This was merely a ruse, but Mama did not want the child to consider that Annamarie herself was the true project of the day. The weird energy of the awful, ancient house had combined with the child's own latent gifts, attracting or creating a … thing. The thing came every night, and seemed to grow and fluctuate with the child's moods. It was intriguing, and unexpected, and Mama thought Annamarie might even have an early breakthrough, gaining a measure of control over her aura—most of the children in the Endeavor did not have any kind of control until they reached puberty. After weeks of monitoring it, she'd realized that the toy was somehow amplifying Annamarie's aural energies, and Mama decided that taking it would present the child with a fascinating new challenge.

It was not strictly prohibited in the Endeavor; side projects were allowed as long as they could be justified.

Annamarie spent a spare minute sulking before retreating in defeat; the Mama did not respond to this tactic.

Annamarie looked under her bed again, and in her closet. She was not, as a rule, a messy child, being rather precocious and having a strict Mama in the bargain. It was all the more mysterious that she couldn't find the toy, to which she had a deep attachment. She'd awakened from her nap to find it missing, and had looked all around their large and drafty house without a successful reunion with her lost Chorley.

At dinner Mama asked, "Did you look for your toy?"

"Yes, Mama." Annamarie was subdued.

Mama looked up from her soup and her newsscreen. "Did you find it?"

"No, Mama."

"Hmm. Well, I suppose you're too old for it, anyway."

This was grievously unfair, but Annamarie knew better than to remark upon it. Although she had an excellent vocabulary for a six-year-old, she could not explain to Mama that the stuffed toy had been painstakingly imbued with protective magic for the last four years, and that there were likely to be dire consequences if she were to retire to bed without it tonight. The spaces beneath the bed and within the wardrobe appeared to be perfectly mundane during daylight hours, but were in fact deep and dangerous repositories for the most nightmarish of creatures once darkness fell.

While she wanted to wail and kick her heels against the floor, Annamarie knew it would do no good; instead, she retreated to her bedroom. She looked around the familiar space, fighting the tears that threatened to fall down her plump cheeks.

She had a small desk, suitable to her short form, upon which she'd accumulated an assortment of electronic gadgets and loose ends from Mama's workshop, the yard, and the shadowy corners of the house. Annamarie had collected circuit boards since she liked the dark green shine of them, and countless wires, and other odds and ends, mostly gathered because of their interesting shapes.

There was a small, high window opposite the door, with a tattered pink curtain that hung limply over it. The curtain matched the quilt on the bed, and those two items were the beginning and end of any bright color in the room, except for, on a shelf over her bed, three other stuffed animals: a parrot, an anteater, and a jaguar. They had never held the special place in her heart which was reserved for the Chorley (named after the young elephant in the bedtime stories her Papa used to tell her).

She had two hours before bedtime, during which she was expected to study or, at the very most, quietly play. Mama was not supposed to be disturbed except during Meeting Times. Mama did not like other interruptions.

Annamarie pulled out her box of circuit boards, and a fistful of wires, and a small screwdriver she'd taken from the kitchen toolbox, and imitated the air of quiet contemplation Mama wore while she did her tinkering.

The girl frowned; she was missing something.

After a moment, she stood on her bed and pulled the other stuffed animals down to the floor with her. "I haven't knew you as long as my Chorley," she said quite solemnly, "but I still love you." She tapped her fingers against her lips, an uncommonly grown-up gesture. "I think you need to be boosted."

She selected a box-cutter—spirited away from Mama's worktable weeks ago—and ripped open the back of the jaguar without hesitation. Annamarie began to play intensely and with great purpose.

Mama, watching from the monitor, did not interrupt her child at bedtime. She was pleased and fascinated by this turn of events, which she had not anticipated, and she took notes for an hour, watching the child's selections and choices, enjoying the way the child mimicked her own work habits. The thaumo-meter hummed happily, measuring the surging energy around the child. Mama watched until the girl went to bed on her own initiative, the three newly modified stuffed animals arranged around her.

The thing that came in the night was perhaps more hungry than inherently evil, but still terrifying to little Annamarie. It oozed into the cracks created by darkness, nesting beneath the bed or curling in the closet. An unwary heel could be grabbed, tugged, and nibbled, if a dash to the bathroom was not properly executed.

The Chorley had protected her. The toy was alive with four years of devoted love; it was a powerful talisman against the thing, which was, after all, only acting according to its own nature. The Chorley repelled it, sent it scuttling for easier prey in other drafty houses. But now the Chorley was gone, and Annamarie had had to make do on short notice.

Mama straightened her glasses, ran her hands through her short-clipped hair, and turned on the dozen monitors which measured everything from the temperature of the room to the ectoplasmic content of the local atmosphere.

The other Mamas had much less to deal with. None of them had gotten stuck in a dark old house full of eaves and topped with crenellations—one variable too many, she'd argued, but been overruled—and most of the other Mamas still had their Papas around to help with their experiments. This Papa had gotten sentimental, protective of the innocent little girl, and that would not do. He'd been retired, peacefully enough. But then he'd tried to come back for Annamarie, and now Mama didn't know where he was, or if they'd even let him live.

She snorted to herself, turning off her computer screen and powering down her laptop for the night. She had a few hours of peace before the child woke. Annamarie was largely self-sufficient, but still required some persuasion in order to get her up and prepared to log in to her morning classes. Mama needed to sleep, but first she went through her own nightly ritual—which involved tea and a night light and a particular quilt, and which she never, ever would have admitted to performing to any of the other Mamas. She did not share anything with them beyond her notes on the child.

When Mama was fast asleep, and Annamarie tossed and turned beneath the surface of consciousness, the thing that came in the night began to ooze and creep into the girl's room. It had, as it always did, bypassed the lonely rooms of the house, and it moved by instinct away from the Mama's nightlight.

It slithered into the dark, cramped corner of the little girl's closet, watching her sleep. She was sweaty, muttering to herself and twitching—the best time, when it could invade the dreams and feed on the terror. An unwary foot was all well and good, but the thing that came in the night preferred fear to flesh. It liked to play with its food.

The child's talisman was gone: its bright blue glow, its glowering eyes, were not there to ward and guard the child. The thing that came in the night moved forward, undulating out of the closet, claws scraping into the cracks of the floorboards.

But it paused mid-rear before pouncing, studying the child on her bed more carefully. There was something wrong... something different.

The thing hissed, a slow angry boil of frustration and irritation.

Here were three new champions; and while they did not shine brightly, they cast their own faint glow through the room, and the edges of their light were painful to the thing that came in the night. They were nowhere near as strong as the Chorley, but they were vigilant, and there were three of them, and they were full of the love and playful energy of the child. Of course, Annamarie was extraordinary—or she would not have been chosen and taken for the Endeavor— and the toys were only one of the ways that her gift had manifested. That bright curiosity burned into something real, something that could affect the world in unexpected ways: it was exactly what the Mamas were trying to measure and control, with limited success. And now that power had been transferred into the toys, giving them a smaller measure of the child's aura, and granting her a sunny protection even as she slumbered.

The thing was forced to retreat, and it went, simmering with fury.

The Mama was unbearably smug during the conference call that took place during the early morning hours. She had every confidence that she understood the energies she'd measured.

"And she received no guidance from you on the matter?" the GrandMama asked.

"None at all," Mama assured her with a sniff. "She created three new guardians. All weaker than the one that's been soaking up her energy this whole time, but it was enough to get that... thing to leave her alone."

Another one of the Mamas spoke, hesitant. She was a new Mama, on her first child. "And you're certain that Annamarie doesn't suspect your part in any of this?"

"Of course not!" Mama said, though she did not really consider her answer before she said it. It had never even occurred to her as a possibility. Of course, the girl was precocious; all of the children were extraordinary. That was the whole point of the Endeavor. But they were still children, and Annamarie was only beginning to develop her talents.

"Keep a sharp eye on her," the GrandMama said. "The... thing is still a new development. We don't want your situation to go awry again."

The Mama schooled her face carefully, though she wanted to scowl. There had been no need to use that last word. This experiment was completely different, and Annamarie was far more talented than the last child the Mama had raised. It was hardly her fault that the last experiment had been abbreviated; of course, the child had died, so there was nothing that could be done about it except to move on. "I will certainly monitor the situation and present all my findings," she said. "On the child and the... thing."

She set aside her feelings of unease after the call. Certainly, there were more variables here than she had wanted, but she would work with what she was given, and she would be promoted within the Endeavor. If Annamarie lived, perhaps Mama could even move up with her. After all, she was the one who had thought of this experiment, and it looked like it might be just the emotional push the girl needed to advance her thaumatronics skills. If not with Annamarie, perhaps next time she could still begin with an older child, already aware of their aura; Mama had earned that much by now, surely. No more shepherding babies through their formative years. That would be a nice change.

For her part, when Annamarie woke, the girl was rested and relieved. The thing in the night had not gotten her, and her nightmares had been mild, even without her Chorley. She hugged her toys tightly in gratitude, and then got herself dressed and found breakfast and waited for Mama to log her into her class.

The toys were left to rest on the neatly-made bed, rather than the shelf above, and they were pleased with their change in status. It was not every day that a toy was elevated to best and beloved, and now that all three of them were now on the bed, well, they could not help but be pleased with themselves.

After her classes, and after Annamarie finished her walk—ten times around the yard, no more, no less—she took her nap with all three toys cuddled in her arms. None of them were particularly large, and with the modifications she'd made, they all had a few sharp edges and pokey bits. The girl didn't mind; she loved them all the more now that she'd made it through a night with them.

When she woke she had a little while before Meeting Time. Mama was busy in her office. She was very pleasant today, and had given Annamarie a cookie when she finished lessons. After her nap, Annamarie had an odd idea.

"Are you sure?" she asked the anteater, who seemed the wisest of the three.

The stuffed toy did not answer out loud, but Annamarie nodded reluctant understanding nonetheless.

Taking the jaguar under her elbow for courage, she crept out of her room, avoiding the creaking floorboards and slipping through Mama's bedroom door, opening it just shy of where it let out a long creaking groan. She rarely came in here; it was a cold room, always clean and tidy but never comfortable. Mama's bed was small, like her own, and although the room was much larger than Annamarie's, there was scarcely any more furniture in it.

Annamarie stopped, listening. She thought she heard a soft rustling from the darkness beneath the bed. She gripped the jaguar extra tight around the middle; the jaguar did not mind. Annamarie took comfort from his steady, stealthy presence, and edged around the room toward the closet.

This door let out a soft whine and Annamarie stopped with her head cocked, listening for Mama. She shivered and took one of the deep good breaths, and then she looked up on the top shelf of the closet.

There was her Chorley, carelessly flung so that it had toppled over on its side and lay on both of its own big, floppy ears. Annamarie let out a little sniffle at this pathetic sight. She reached her arms up, the jaguar still grasped by one ankle, and stood on tippy toes, but came nowhere close to reaching the stuffed elephant.

Annamarie left Mama's bedroom door propped open and crept back to her own room, sliding her bare feet along the rough floorboards where she knew they wouldn't creak. She gulped for air, back in her own room, and crushed the jaguar against her cheek for a final boost to her courage. Then she took the parrot and left her room again.

She paused outside Mama's office door; Mama was on the phone with someone, talking in one of the other languages. She was leaned back in her chair, with one arm over her eyes. While Annamarie watched, Mama straightened and lowered her arm, and her eyes brushed past the doorway where Annamarie stood.

But she didn't see Annamarie. She swiveled to face her desk, and Annamarie wrenched herself along.

She hovered uncertainly at Mama's closet door, looking at her Chorley. The one eye she could see—a scratched black button peeking over the edge of the shelf—implored Annamarie for rescue.

The little girl braced her feet evenly beneath her and tossed the parrot up toward the top of the closet. It was an impossible throw in the too-narrow space between the door and the shelf, and the elephant rested heavily and certainly on that shelf. Yet an instant later, both toys came tumbling back down and the girl caught them with no more than a muffled, feathery thump.

She heard a clunk and a clatter from Mama's office, and whirled around, clutching her toys. Another moment passed without a sound, and she tiptoed to the door, edging around Mama's dresser. When she passed the ugly little porcelain nightlight, the elephant's trunk snagged on the cord, and the thing tipped over with a *crunchthud*. The girl winced and froze. She set the light back upright, and fled to her own room. She did not tell Mama about the nightlight—Mama had taken her Chorley, after all, and could not be trusted—and there were no monitors in Mama's room, so, in later review, the other Mamas would never fully understand what happened that night.

When Mama came and got her for Meeting Time, the girl was on the floor, contentedly playing the coding game on her tablet. The parrot, anteater, and jaguar were ranged around her, as though they were participating in the programming.

"Make your bed more tidily tomorrow, Annamarie," Mama said. "It's very lumpy today."

"Yes, Mama," the girl said.

"Go and wash your hands and join me for supper," Mama said.

"Yes, Mama." She leapt up from the floor, grinning, but Mama had already started down the hall.

They ate a quiet dinner, and when they were done, Mama went back to her office and the girl went back to her room to do her homework.

When she went to bed that night, Mama was disgruntled to find that the bulb of her nightlight was not working. She gave a soft, muttered curse; she didn't have any spares. She'd have to get one tomorrow. Still, she was a grown woman, she reasoned. How much could a child's boogeyman really bother her?

At least she thought so, for a few more hours.

Annamarie slept blissfully well that night, with her modified toys ranged around her and the Chorley hugged tight in her arms. In the morning she woke late.

GrandMama was there. Annamarie did not like her. "Where's Mama?"

The old woman sniffed. "She's not... well. She won't be looking after you anymore."

"Will I get to see Papa?" A surge of excitement rippled through her.

"No," GrandMama said quickly. "No, you'll have a new Mama. I've come to take you to her." She glared around Annamarie's room; she found no fault with it, but still did not like the room... or the house, for that matter.

It took next to no time for Annamarie to dress and gather her things, hastily arranging her toys beneath her clothing. GrandMama recalled, uneasily, the Mama's report on how Annamarie had used her toys to channel her growing power... but with so many changes today, she would not take the toys from the child now. No, a smooth transition would be best; once everything else was under control, a new Mama could get the girl in line. GrandMama offered a hand, which the child reached to take, but a yucky jolt went through Annamarie's arm. She pulled back to grip her suitcase instead.

"Are you ready, then, child?" GrandMama asked.

Annamarie nodded. Mama had always told her that she had to obey GrandMama, but Mama had taken her Chorley. Annamarie made a secret promise to her Chorley that she would not trust GrandMama, not ever. Or the new Mama either. Annamarie walked down the steps after GrandMama: suitcase dragging behind her, and, tucked carefully into the bag over her shoulder, her Chorley.

See Rachel Ayers's story "The Chorley" online at Metaphorosis.
If you liked it, leave a comment. Authors love that!
Remember to subscribe to our e-mail updates so you'll know when new stories are posted.

About the story

I had this image in my head of the valiant teddy bear defending a sleeping child from the monster in the dark... and I wondered what would happen if the toy hero were taken away. (Which I guess makes me the Mama in this scenario...)

A question for the author

Q: What distracts you?

A: The next idea... It's hard to focus on one story at a time when the next idea is — oooh, shiny squirrels!

About the author

Rachel Ayers lives in Alaska, where she writes cabaret shows, daydreams, and looks at mountains a lot. She has a degree in Library and Information Science, which comes in handy at odd hours, and she shares speculative poetry and flash fiction (and cat pictures) at patreon.com/richlayers

@richlayers

Copyright

Title information

Metaphorosis July 2020

ISSN: 2573-136X (online)
ISBN: 978-1-64076-173-5 (e-book)
ISBN: 978-1-64076-174-2 (paperback)

Copyright

Authors also retain copyrights to all other material in the anthology.

Works of fiction

This book contains works of fiction. Characters, dialogue, places, organizations, incidents, and events portrayed in the works are fictional and are products of the author's imagination or used fictitiously. Any resemblance to actual persons, places, organizations, or events is coincidental.

All rights reserved

The authors and artists worked hard to create this work for your enjoyment. Please respect their work and their rights by using only authorized copies. If you would like to share this material with others, please buy them a copy.

Moral rights asserted

Each author whose work is included in this book has asserted their moral rights, including the right to be identified as the author of their respective work(s).

Publisher

Metaphorosis

a magazine of speculative fiction

Metaphorosis Magazine is an imprint of
Metaphorosis Publishing
Neskowin, OR, USA

www.metaphorosis.com

Discounts available

Substantial discounts are available for educational institutions, including writing workshops. Discounts are also available for quantity purchases. For details, contact Metaphorosis at metaphorosis.com/about

Metaphorosis Publishing

Metaphorosis offers beautifully written science fiction and fantasy. Our imprints include:

Metaphorosis Magazine
Plant Based Press
Verdage

You can also find us:
@MetaphorosisMag, @MetaphorosisRev, @Metaphorosis
www.facebook.com/metaphorosis

Help keep Metaphorosis running by supporting us at
Patreon.com/metaphorosis

See more about some of our books on the following pages.

Metaphorosis

a magazine of speculative fiction

Metaphorosis is an online speculative fiction magazine dedicated to quality writing. We publish an original story every week, along with author bios, interviews, and notes on story origins.

We also publish monthly print and e-book issues, as well as yearly Best of and Complete anthologies.

Come and see us online at magazine.Metaphorosis.com

Metaphorosis: Best of 2019

The best science fiction and fantasy stories from *Metaphorosis* magazine's fourth year.

Metaphorosis 2019

All the stories from *Metaphorosis* magazine's fourth year. Fifty-two great SFF stories.

Metaphorosis:
Best of 2018

The best science fiction and fantasy stories from *Metaphorosis* magazine's third year.

Metaphorosis
2018

All the stories from *Metaphorosis* magazine's third year. Fifty-two great SFF stories.

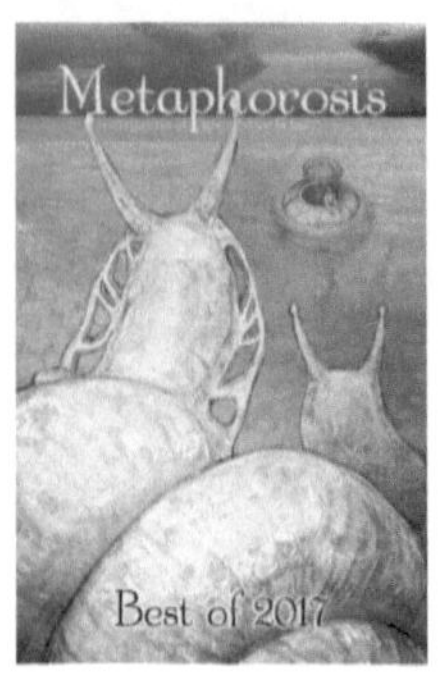

Metaphorosis:
Best of 2017

The best science fiction and fantasy stories from *Metaphorosis* magazine's *second* year.

Metaphorosis
2017

All the stories from *Metaphorosis* magazine's second year. Fifty-three great SFF stories.

Metaphorosis:
Best of 2016

The best science fiction and fantasy stories from *Metaphorosis* magazine's first year.

Metaphorosis
2016

Almost all the stories from *Metaphorosis* magazine's first year.

Plant Based Press

Vegan-friendly science fiction and fantasy, including an annual anthology of the year's best SFF stories.

Best Vegan SFF of 2019

The best vegan-friendly science fiction and fantasy stories of 2019!

Best Vegan SFF of 2018

The best vegan-friendly science fiction and fantasy stories of 2018!

Best Vegan SFF of 2017

The best vegan-friendly science fiction and fantasy stories of 2017!

Best Vegan SFF of 2016

The best vegan-friendly science fiction and fantasy stories of 2016!

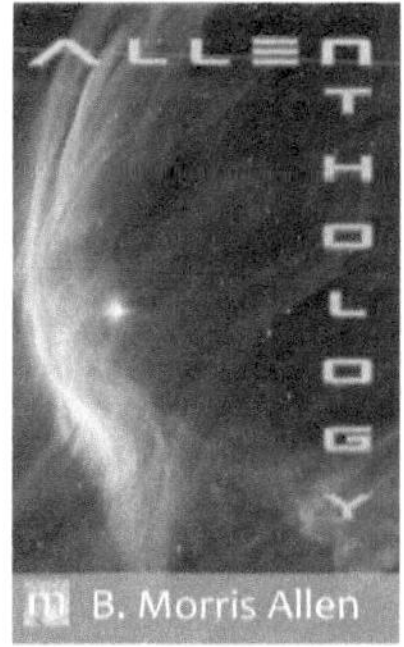

Susurrus

A darkly romantic story of magic, love, and suffering.

Allenthology: Volume I

A quarter century of SFF, including the full contents of the collections *Tocsin, Start with Stones,* and *Metaphorosis.*

Verdage

Science fiction and fantasy books for writers – full of great stories, often with an additional focus on the craft of speculative fiction writing.

Score

an SFF symphony

What if stories were written like music? *Score* is an anthology of varied stories arranged to follow an emotional score from the heights of joy to the depths of despair – but always with a little hope shining through.

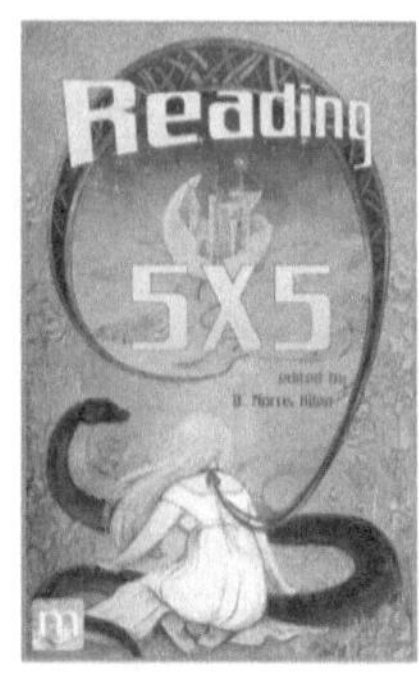

Reading 5X5

Five stories, five times

Twenty-five SFF authors, five base stories, five versions of each – see how different writers take on the same material, with stories in contemporary and high fantasy, soft and hard SF, and a mysterious 'other' category.

Reading 5X5

Writers' Edition

All the stories from the regular, readers' edition, plus two extra stories, the story seed, and authors' notes on writing. Over 100 pages of additional material specifically aimed at writers.